Back by Popular Demand

A collector's edition of favorite titles from one of the world's best-loved romance authors. Harlequin is proud to bring back these sought-after titles and present them as one cherished collection.

BETTY NEELS:
COLLECTOR'S EDITION

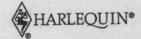

HARLEQUIN®

Betty Neels spent her childhood and youth in Devonshire before training as a nurse and midwife. She was an army nursing sister during the war, married a Dutchman and subsequently lived in Holland for fourteen years. She now lives with her husband in Dorset, and has a daughter and grandson. Her hobbies are reading, animals, old buildings and, of course, writing. Betty started to write on retirement from nursing, incited by a lady in a library bemoaning the lack of romantic novels.

Mrs. Neels is always delighted to receive fan letters, but would truly appreciate it if they could be directed to Harlequin Mills & Boon Ltd., 18-24 Paradise Road, Richmond, Surrey, TW9 1SR, England.

Books by Betty Neels

HARLEQUIN ROMANCE

BETTY NEELS

THE MOON FOR LAVINIA

COLLECTOR'S EDITION

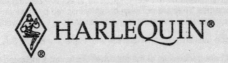

HARLEQUIN®

TORONTO • NEW YORK • LONDON
AMSTERDAM • PARIS • SYDNEY • HAMBURG
STOCKHOLM • ATHENS • TOKYO • MILAN • MADRID
PRAGUE • WARSAW • BUDAPEST • AUCKLAND

ISBN 0-373-63104-9

THE MOON FOR LAVINIA

First North American Publication 1999.

Copyright © 1975 by Betty Neels.

Visit us at www.romance.net

Printed in U.S.A.

CHAPTER ONE

IT WAS QUIET now that the day's lists were over; the operating theatre, gleaming with near-sterile cleanliness and no longer lighted by its great shadowless lamp, looked a very different place from the hive of ordered activity it had been since early morning, for now the surgeons and anaesthetists had gone, as well as Theatre Sister and most of her staff; indeed, the department held but one occupant, a nurse sitting on a stool in front of one of the trolleys, sorting instruments with swift precision.

She was a small, neat person, a little plump, and with a face which was neither plain nor pretty, although when she laughed her hazel eyes widened and twinkled and her too large mouth curved charmingly. It was a pity that she laughed all too seldom, and now, deep in thought as she worked, she looked rather on the plain side and sad with it. She finished her task, tidied everything away neatly and began a final inspection of the theatre before she went off duty. It was a Sunday evening, and for some reason one staff nurse was considered sufficient to be on duty after six o'clock; presumably on the principle that it being a Sunday, people would be less prone to require emergency surgery, and for once this had been proved right; the evening hours, spent in doing the necessary chores had been too quiet, so that Lavinia Hawkins had had time to think, which was a pity, for she had nothing pleasant to think about.

She went along to take off her gown, threw it into the laundry bin, and then sat down again, this time on the only chair the changing room possessed. The June sun, still warm and bright, streamed in through the window, and she could hear, very faintly, the subdued hum of the London evening traffic, most of it returning from an outing to the sea. It would have been a perfect day for them, thought Lavinia without envy, although she wasn't very happy herself; it was a good thing that she was going to Aunt Gwyneth's in two days' time and would have the chance to talk to Peta, her young sister—perhaps they would be able to plan something. Quite forgetful of the time, she took Peta's letter from her pocket and read it once more.

Peta was dreadfully unhappy; when their mother had died, more than a year ago now, and Aunt Gwyneth had offered her a home, Lavinia had been grateful for her help. There was no money, the annuity her mother had lived upon died with her; her father had died a number of years earlier, and although she herself had been self-supporting and had even been able to help out with Peta's school fees, her sister's education had been at a stage when to make changes in it would have been nothing short of criminal. For one thing, Peta was clever and working for her O levels, and for another, Lavinia was only too well aware that a sound education for her sister was essential if she was to be self-supporting too, so that when her mother died Lavinia accepted her aunt's offer with an eager gratitude which she had since come to regret.

It hadn't worked out at all. Aunt Gwyneth was a widow and comfortably off, living in a large house on the outskirts of Cuckfield which was run by a highly efficient housekeeper, leaving her free to indulge her passion for bridge and committee meetings. Lavinia had honestly thought that she would be glad to have Peta to live with her; she had no children of her own and Peta was a darling, pretty and sweet-tempered and anxious to please. It was after she had been at Cuckfield for several months that Lavinia began to sense that something was wrong, but it had taken her a long time to persuade Peta to tell her what was amiss and when, at last, she had got her to talk about it it was to discover that it wasn't just the natural unhappiness she felt at the loss of her mother—life wasn't fun, she confided to Lavinia; her aunt had discovered that having a teenager in the house had its drawbacks. True, Peta was at school all day, but at the week-ends and during the holidays she was made to feel a nuisance, and whenever she suggested that she might spend a few days with Lavinia, there were always good reasons why she shouldn't...

Lavinia, her arm round her sister's slim shoulders, had frowned. 'Darling, you should have told me,' she had said. 'I could have spoken to Aunt Gwyneth,' but even as she uttered the words she had known that it wasn't going to be as easy as all that. Peta was due to take her O levels in a week or two's time, and the plan had been for her to stay on at school and try for her A levels in a couple of years. Even if Lavinia had had a flat of her own, which she hadn't, it would still be difficult, for there would still be the question of where Peta should go to school and how would she ever afford the fees? 'Look,' she had advised, 'could you hang on for another year or two, love—just until you've got those A levels? I'm to have Sister Drew's job when she retires, and that's less than a year now; I'll save every penny I can and find a flat.'

And Peta had agreed. That had been barely a week ago, and now here was her letter, begging Lavinia to take her away from Aunt Gwyneth,

promising incoherently to stay until the exam re-
sults were out, if only she would take her away...
Lavinia folded the letter up once more and put it
in her pocket. She had a headache from worrying
about what was to be done, for whatever it was, it
would have to be done quickly, and at the moment
she had no ideas at all. She went down to supper,
turning over in her mind a variety of ideas, none
of which, unfortunately, stood up to close scrutiny.

Most of her friends were already in the canteen,
queueing for baked beans on toast and cups of tea.
They shared a table, making the beans last as long
as possible while they discussed the day's work. It
was as they lingered over the last dregs of their tea
that Shirley Thompson from Women's Surgical declared herself to be completely fed up with that
ward, its Sister, the patients, and indeed the whole
hospital. 'I'm sick of Jerrold's,' she declared. 'I'm
going to look for another job. I've got the *Nursing
Mirror* in my room, let's go and make a pot of tea
and find me a new job.'

No one quite believed her; for one thing, she
was going steady with one of the house surgeons;
and for another, she made this same announcement
every few months, but it was too soon for bed and
there wasn't much else to do; they trooped from
the canteen and across to the Nurses' Home, where
they crowded into the Sisters' lift, strictly forbid-

den, but no one was likely to see them on a Sunday evening, anyway, and besides, everyone did it and hoped not to be caught, and once on the top floor they disposed themselves around Shirley's room, ready to drink more tea and give her their not very serious advice.

They were debating, in a lighthearted manner, the advantages of nursing an octogenarian recovering from a fractured femur in Belgravia, as opposed to a post as school nurse in a boarding establishment in Cumberland, when the *Nursing Mirror* came into Lavinia's hands. She glanced through it idly and turning a page had her eye instantly caught by a large advertisement headed simply 'Amsterdam'. She read it carelessly, and then, struck by a blindingly super idea, very carefully.

Registered nurses wanted, said the advertisement, with theatre experience and at a salary which was quite fabulous. Knowledge of Dutch was unnecessary; lessons could be arranged, and provided the applicant proved suitable and wished to remain for a period of not less than six months, outside accommodation would be found for her. Lavinia, never very good at her sums, got out her pen and did some basic arithmetic on the underside of her uniform skirt. Supposing, just supposing that the job was all it said it was, if she could get somewhere to live, Peta could live with her, for they could manage on that salary if they were careful. Of course, the plan was completely crazy; Peta's education would come to a halt, but then, Lavinia feared, it would do that if Peta stayed at Cuckfield; her sister's vehemence was clear enough in her letter, it would be awful if she were to run away... Lavinia shuddered just thinking about it—and wouldn't it be better to have her sister under her eye and once she had settled down, devise some plan whereby she might finish her education? She calculated quickly; Peta was only a week or two under sixteen when she could leave school quite legitimately, so there would be no trouble there, and although she knew nothing about education in Holland there would surely be some way of completing her studies.

When the gathering broke up, she begged the journal from Shirley and before she went to bed that night, applied for the job.

She went down to Cuckfield two days later and found Peta alone in the house, waiting for her, and when she saw her sister's face any doubts which she had been secretly harbouring about a plan which common sense told her was a little short of hare-brained were put at rest. Peta was dreadfully unhappy and Lavinia, ten years her senior, felt a motherly urge to set things right as quickly as possible.

Aunt Gwyneth was out and would be back for lunch, and, the housekeeper told Lavinia, Mrs Turner was looking forward to a nice chat before her niece went back that evening.

Lavinia sighed. The nice chats were really nothing but questions and answers—her aunt asked the questions; rather rude ones usually, and she answered them with a polite vagueness which invariably annoyed her elderly relation, for her aunt, while professing a fondness for Peta, had never liked her. Even as a small girl she had refused to be browbeaten by her father's elder sister and her hectoring manner had left her quite unimpressed; it had never worried her father either, who had brushed it aside like a troublesome swarm of flies, but her mother, a gentle creature like Peta, had often wilted under her sister-in-law's tongue. Lavinia, made of sterner stuff, had refused to be intimidated, and Aunt Gwyneth, annoyed at this, took her petty revenge by never inviting her to stay at her home, either for her holidays or her free days. She was too clever to do this openly, of course, but somehow, when holidays came round, the bedrooms were being decorated, or her aunt was going away herself or felt too poorly to have visitors, and as for her days off, invariably at teatime Lavinia would be asked which train she intended to catch and some reference would be made as to her eagerness to get back to Jerrold's, in order, presumably, to plunge into a hectic round of gaiety with every doctor in the place.

This veiled assumption of her popularity with the men was something which amused Lavinia very much; her aunt knew well enough that she had no men friends; she got on very well with the doctors and students she worked with, but none of them had shown her any decided preference and she doubted if they ever would; she had no looks to speak of and a quiet manner which, while encouraging young men to confide in her, did nothing to catch their fancy.

They were sitting together in the sitting room having their morning coffee when Peta burst out: 'Lavinia, I can't stay here—I simply can't! Aunt Gwyneth keeps telling me how good she's been to me—and you, though I can't think how—she makes me feel like a—a pauper. I know we haven't any money, but she is our aunt and our only relation, and do you know what she said? That in a year or two, when I've finished school and am earning my living, you'll have to leave your job in hospital and be her companion, because she'll need someone by then and it's only natural that you should be the one because she's given me a home.'

She added unhappily: 'Lavinia, what are we going to do?'

Lavinia refilled their coffee cups. 'I'll tell you, darling.'

She outlined her plan simply, making light of its obvious drawbacks, glad that Peta hadn't spotted them in her excitement. 'So you see, Peta, everything will be super, only you must promise to stay here and take your O levels and say nothing about our plan to anyone. I haven't heard from these people yet, but I think I've got a good chance of getting a job. I'll have to give a month's notice at Jerrold's—give me a couple of weeks to find my way about, and I'll come for you. Could you stick it for just a little longer?'

Peta nodded. 'Darling Lavinia, of course I can. You're sure we can live on what you'll earn in Amsterdam? I could get a job…'

'Yes, love, I know, but I think we'll be able to manage. I'd rather you went on with your studies—perhaps if you could learn Dutch, enough to help you get a job later on? UNO and all that,' she added vaguely, and looked at the clock. 'Aunt Gwyneth will be here very soon, let's talk about something else so that we're just as usual when she comes. Tell me about school.'

Their aunt found them poring over school books, arguing cheerfully about applied physics although

Lavinia knew almost nothing about the subject. She got up to greet her aunt and received a chilly peck on her cheek while the lady studied her. 'You must be twenty-six,' she observed. 'Such a pity you have no looks, Lavinia. How fortunate that you took up nursing as a career, although waiting until you were twenty-two seems to me to have been a needless waste of time—you could have been a ward Sister by now.'

Lavinia thought of several answers to this unfortunate remark, but none of them were very polite; they went in to lunch in a little flurry of polite and meaningless remarks.

Lunch was excellent; Aunt Gwyneth enjoyed her comforts and made sure that she had them, although she pointed out during dessert that her nieces were lucky girls indeed to enjoy the benefits of her generosity. Lavinia, still peevish about her aunt's remark about her lack of looks, felt an urge to throw her trifle across the table at her. No wonder poor little Peta was fed up; anything would be better than putting up with the succession of snide remarks which tripped off her relation's tongue. For once she answered with relief when she was asked at what time she was returning to hospital.

'I daresay you have plans for the evening,' said Aunt Gwyneth, 'and I'm not so selfish as to delay you in any way. After tea, you say? That is ad-

mirable, for I have a small bridge party this evening, and Peta has a great deal of studying to do
in preparation for her exams.' Her two listeners
expected her to add a rider to the effect that if it
hadn't been for her, there would have been no possibility of exams, but she contented herself with a
smug smile.

So Lavinia went back after tea, not liking to
leave Peta, but seeing no alternative, but at least
she was heartened to see how much more cheerful
her sister was. They parted under their aunt's eye,
so that all Lavinia could say was: 'See you next
week, Peta—if I may come down, Aunt?' she
added politely, and received a gracious nod of as-
sent.

There was a letter for her on Monday morning,
asking her to go for an interview, either that afternoon or on the following morning, and as luck
would have it she had been given a split duty because Sister wanted the evening, and the morning's
list was too heavy for them both to be off duty at
the same time. She changed into a plain coffee-
coloured linen dress, coiled her long hair with care,
made up her face, and caught a bus; only as she
was going through the open door of the hotel
where the interviews were to be held did she pause
to think what she was doing, and by then it was
too late. There were a dozen or more girls waiting,

some of them younger than she, and most of them prettier; there was a possibility of her not getting a job after all; she hadn't expected quite so many applicants.

She was brooding over this when her turn came, and she found herself on the other side of the door, invited to sit down by a middle-aged lady sitting at a table, and stared at by the two people on either side of her. A man, a large comfortable-looking man in his fifties, and another woman, young this time—not much older than herself and very fair with a wholesome out-of-doors look about her.

The lady in the middle opened the interview with a pleasant: 'Miss Hawkins? We are pleased that you could come and see us. My name is Platsma—Mevrouw Platsma, and this is Juffrouw Smid and also Professor van Leek, who is the Medical Director of our hospital in Amsterdam. Miss Smid is the Sister-in-Charge of the theatre unit.' She paused to smile. 'What are your qualifications, Miss Hawkins?'

Lavinia gave them without trying to make more of them than they were.

'And your reasons for wishing to work with us?'

She told them the truth, fined down to the facts and without enlarging upon Aunt Gwyneth. 'I think I could live on the salary you offer and have my sister to live with me, something we both would like very much—I can't do that here because I can't afford a flat—I live in at Jerrold's. I should like to live in Amsterdam too; I've never been out of England.'

'You like your work?'

'Very much.'

'You are accustomed to scrub?'

'Yes. There are four theatres in our unit, I work in General Surgery and take most of the cases when Sister is off duty.'

'You have no objection to us referring to your superiors at the hospital?'

'No, none at all. If I should be considered for the job, I should have to give a month's notice.'

They all three smiled at her and Mevrouw Platsma said: 'Thank you, Miss Hawkins, we will let you know at the earliest opportunity.'

She went back to Jerrold's feeling uncertain; her qualifications were good, she would be given excellent references she felt sure, but then so might the other girls who had been there. She told herself sensibly to forget about it, something easily done, as it turned out, for there was an emergency perforation that evening, followed by a ruptured appendix. She went off duty too tired to do more than eat a sketchy supper, have a bath, and go to bed.

There was a letter by the first post in the morning. She had got the job. She did an excited little jig in the scrubbing-up room, begged permission to go to the office at once, and presented herself, rather breathless still, before the Principal Nursing Officer's desk.

Miss Mint heard her out, expressed regret that she should want to leave, but added in the same breath that it was a splendid thing to broaden one's mind when young and that should Lavinia wish to return to Jerrold's at some future date, she could be sure of a post—if there was one vacant—at any time. She finished this encouraging speech by observing that probably she had some holidays due to her, in which case she should be able to leave sooner.

Lavinia becamed at her. 'Oh, Miss Mint, I have—a week. I knew you would understand about me wanting to go somewhere where I could have Peta with me…I only hope I'll make a success of it.'

Miss Mint smiled. 'I can think of no reason why you shouldn't,' she said encouragingly. 'Come and see me before you go, Staff Nurse. I shall of course supply references when they are required.'

Lavinia went through the rest of the day in a daze, doing her work with her usual efficiency while she thought about her new job. She spent a good deal of her lunch hour writing to accept the post, and only restrained herself by a great effort from writing to Peta too, but there was always the danger that their aunt would read the letter, and telephoning would be just as chancy; she should have thought of that sooner and arranged for her sister to telephone her on her way home from school. Now the news would have to wait until she paid her weekly visit on Saturday.

The days flashed by; she received particulars of her job, how she was to travel, and the day on which she was expected, as well as the gratifying news that her references were entirely satisfactory. She had a few pounds saved; the temptation to spend some of them on new clothes was very strong, so on her morning off she went along to Oxford Street.

It was a splendid day and the gay summer clothes in the shop windows exactly matched her mood; discarding all sensible ideas about practical rainwear, hard-wearing shoes and colours which wouldn't show the dirt, she plunged recklessly, returning to the Nurses' Home laden with parcels; new sandals—pretty pink ones to match the pink cotton dress and jacket she hadn't been able to resist, a pale green linen skirt with a darling little linen blouse to go with it, and as well as these, a long cardigan which happily matched them both. There was a dress too, pale green silk jersey, and as a sop to her conscience, a raincoat, coffee-coloured and lightweight. She laid everything out on her bed and admired them and tried not to think of all the money she had spent, cheering herself with the thought that she still had something tucked away and enough besides to get her through the first month in Amsterdam before she would be paid. And when Peta joined her, she would buy her some pretty dresses too; Aunt Gwyneth's ideas ran to the serviceable and dull for her niece; the two of them would scour Amsterdam for the sort of clothes girls of Peta's age liked to wear.

Her sister was waiting for her when she got to Cuckfield on Saturday morning and so was their aunt. There was no chance to talk at all until after lunch, and then only for a few minutes while Aunt Gwyneth was telephoning. 'It's OK,' said Lavinia softly. 'I've got the job—I'm going two weeks today. I'll tell Aunt when I come next week, but only that I'm going—nothing about you yet—and don't say anything, love, whatever you do.' She smiled at Peta. 'Try not to look so happy, darling. Tell me about your exams—do you think you did well?'

She didn't stay as long as usual; her aunt had a bridge date directly after tea and was anxious for her to be gone, and a tentative suggestion that she might take Peta out for the evening was met with a number of perfectly feasible reasons why she shouldn't. That was the trouble with Aunt Gwyneth, thought Lavinia crossly, she never flatly refused anything, which made it very hard to argue with her. She wondered, as she went back to London, how her aunt would take the news of her new job.

She thought about it several times during the ensuing week, but theatre was busy and there really wasn't much time to worry about anything else. Saturday, when it came, was another cloudless day. Lavinia, in a rather old cotton dress because she was starting on the business of packing her things, felt cheerful as she walked the short distance from the station to her aunt's house. And her aunt seemed in a good mood too, so that without giving herself time to get nervous, Lavinia broke her news.

It was received with surprising calm. 'Let us hope,' said her aunt ponderously, 'that this new venture will improve your status sufficiently for you to obtain a more senior post later on—it is the greatest pity that you did not take up nursing immediately you left school, for you must be a good deal older than the average staff nurse.'

Lavinia let this pass. It was partly true in any case, though it need not have been mentioned in such unkind terms. Everyone knew quite well why she had stayed at home when she had left school; her mother was alone and Peta was still a small girl, and over and above that, her mother hadn't been strong. She said now, schooling her voice to politeness: 'I don't know about that, Aunt, but the change will be nice and the pay's good.'

'As long as you don't squander it,' replied Aunt Gwyneth tartly. 'But it is a good opportunity for you to see something of the world, I suppose; the time will come when I shall need a companion, as you well know. Peta will be far too young and lively for me, and I shall expect you, Lavinia, to give up your nursing and look after me. It is the least you can do for me after the sacrifices I have made for you both.'

Lavinia forbore from commenting that she had had nothing done for her at all; even holidays and days off had been denied her, and though she was a fair-minded girl, the worthy stockings, edifying books and writing paper she had received so regularly at Christmas and birthdays could hardly be classed as sacrifices. And her aunt could quite well afford to pay for a companion; someone she could bully if she wanted to and who would be able to answer back without the chain of family ties to hold her back. She sighed with deep contentment, thinking of her new job, and her aunt mistaking her reason for sighing, remarked that she was, and always had been, an ungrateful girl.

Lavinia wasn't going to see Peta again before

she left England, although she had arranged to telephone her at a friend's house before she went. She spent the week in making final arrangements, aided, and hindered too, by her many friends. They had a party for her on her last night, with one bottle of sherry between a dozen or more of them, a great many pots of tea and a miscellany of food. There was a great deal of laughing and talking too, and when someone suggested that Lavinia should find herself a husband while she was in Holland, a chorus of voices elaborated the idea. 'Someone rich— good-looking—both—with an enormous house so that they could all come and stay…' The party broke up in peals of laughter. Lavinia was very popular, but no one really believed that she was likely to find herself such a delightful future, and she believed it least of all.

She left the next morning, after a guarded telephone talk with Peta and a noisy send-off from her friends at Jerrold's. She was to go by plane, and the novelty of that was sufficient to keep her interested until the flat coast of Holland appeared beneath them and drove home the fact that she had finally left her safe, rather dull life behind, and for one she didn't know much about. They began to circle Schiphol airport, and she sat rigid. Supposing that after all no one spoke English? Dutch, someone had told her, was a fearful language until you got the hang of it. Supposing that there had been some mistake and when she arrived no one expected her? Supposing the theatre technique was different, even though they had said it wasn't...? She followed the other passengers from the plane, went through Customs and boarded the bus waiting to take her to Amsterdam.

The drive was just long enough to give her time to pull herself together and even laugh a little at her silly ideas. It was a bit late to get cold feet now, anyway, and she had the sudden hopeful feeling that she was going to like her new job very much. She looked about her eagerly as the bus churned its way through the morning traffic in the narrow streets and at the terminal she did as she had been instructed: showed the hospital's address to a hovering taxi-driver, and when he had loaded her luggage into his cab, got in beside it. The new life had begun.

CHAPTER TWO

THE HOSPITAL WAS on the fringe of the city's centre; a large, old-fashioned building, patched here and there with modern additions which its three-hundred-year-old core had easily absorbed. It was tucked away behind the busy main streets, with narrow alleys, lined with tiny, slightly shabby houses, round three sides of it. On the fourth side there was a great covered gateway, left over from a bygone age, which was still wide enough to accommodate the comings and goings of ambulances and other motor traffic.

Lavinia paused to look about her as she got out of the taxi. The driver got out too and set her luggage on the pavement, said something she couldn't understand, and then humped it up the steps of the hospital and left it in the vast porch. Only when he had done this did he tell her how much she needed to pay him. As she painstakingly sorted out the *guldens* he asked: 'You are nurse?' and when she nodded, refused the tip she offered him. London taxi drivers seldom took tips from a nurse either, sometimes they wouldn't even accept a fare— perhaps it was a worldwide custom. She thanked him when he wished her good luck and waited until his broad friendly back had disappeared inside his cab before going through the big glass doors, feeling as though she had lost a friend.

But she need not have felt nervous; no sooner had she peered cautiously through the porter's lodge window than he was there, asking her what she wanted, and when he discovered that she was the expected English nurse, he summoned another porter, gave him incomprehensible instructions, said, just as the taxi driver had said: 'Good luck,' and waved her into line behind her guide. She turned back at the last moment, remembering her luggage, and was reassured by his cheerful: 'Baggage is OK.'

The porter was tall and thin and walked fast; Lavinia, almost trotting to keep up with him, had scant time in which to look around her. She had an impression of dark walls, a tiled floor and endless doors on either side of the passages they were traversing so rapidly. Presently they merged into a wider one which in its turn ended at a splendid archway opening on to a vestibule, full of doors. The porter knocked on one of these, opened it and stood on one side of it for her to enter.

The room was small, and seemed smaller because of the woman standing by the window, for she was very large—in her forties, perhaps, with a straight back, a billowing bosom and a long, strong-featured face. Her eyes were pale blue and her hair, drawn back severely from her face, was iron grey. When she smiled, Lavinia thought she was one of the nicest persons she had ever seen.

'Miss Hawkins?' Her voice was as nice as her smile. 'We are glad to welcome you to St Jorus and we hope that you will be happy here.' She nodded towards a small hard chair. 'Will you sit, please?'

Lavinia sat, listening carefully while the Directrice outlined her duties, mentioned off-duty, touched lightly on uniforms, salary and the advisability of taking Dutch lessons and went on: 'You will find that the medical staff speak English and also some of the nurses too—the domestic staff, they will not, but there will be someone to help you for a little while. You will soon pick up a few necessary words, I feel sure.'

She smiled confidently at Lavinia, who smiled back, not feeling confident at all. Certainly she would make a point of starting lessons as soon as possible; she hadn't heard more than a few sentences of Dutch so far, but they had sounded like gibberish.

'You wish to live out, I understand,' went on the Directrice, 'and that will be possible within a week or so, but first you must be quite certain that you want to remain with us, although we should not stand in your way if before then you should decide to return to England.'

'I was thinking of staying for a year,' ventured Lavinia, 'but I'd rather not decide until I've been here a few days, but I do want to make a home for my young sister.'

Her companion looked curious but forbore from pressing for further information, instead she rang the bell on her desk and when a young woman in nurse's uniform but without a cap answered it, she said kindly:

'This is Juffrouw Fiske, my secretary. She will take you over to the Nurses' Home and show you your room. You would like to unpack, and perhaps it would be as well if you went on duty directly after the midday meal. Theatre B, major surgery. There is a short list this afternoon and you will have a chance to find your feet.'

Lavinia thanked her and set off with Juffrouw Fiske through more passages and across a couple of small courtyards, enclosed by high grey walls until they finally came to a door set in one of the— the back door, she was told, to the Home. It gave directly on to a short passage with a door at its end opening on to a wide hall in which was a flight of stairs which they climbed.

'There is a lift,' explained her companion, 'but

you are on the first floor, therefore there is no
need.'

She opened a door only a few yards from the
head of the stairs and invited Lavinia to go in. It
was a pleasant room, tolerably large and very well
furnished, and what was more, her luggage was
there as well as a pile of uniform on the bed.

'We hope that everything fits,' said Juffrouw
Fiske. 'You are small, are you not?' She smiled
widely. 'We are quite often big girls. Someone will
come and take you to your dinner at twelve
o'clock, Miss Hawkins, and I hope that you will
be happy with us.'

Nice people, decided Lavinia, busily unpacking.
She had already decided that she was going to like
the new job—she would like it even better when
she had a home of her own and Peta with her. Of
course, she still had to meet the people she was to
work with, but if they were half as nice as those
she had met already, she felt she need have no
fears about getting on with them.

The uniform fitted very well. She perched the
stiff little cap on top of her tidy topknot and sat
down to wait for whoever was to fetch her.

It was a big, well-built girl, with ash blonde hair
and a merry face. She shook hands with enthusiasm and said: 'Neeltje Haagsma.'

For a moment Lavinia wondered if she was be-

ing asked how she did in Dutch, but the girl put
her right at once. 'My name—we shake hands and
say our names when we meet—that is simple, is it
not?'

Lavinia nodded. 'Lavinia Hawkins. Do I call
you *juffrouw*?'

Neeltje pealed with laughter. 'No, no—you will
call me Neeltje and I will call you Lavinia, only
you must call the Hoofd Zuster, Zuster Smid.'

'And the doctors?' They were making for the
stairs.

'Doctor—easy, is it not? and *chirurgen*—surgeon, is it not?—you will call them Mister this or
Mister that.'

Not so foreign after all, Lavinia concluded happily, and then was forced to change her mind when
they entered an enormous room, packed with
nurses sitting at large tables eating their dinner and
all talking at the tops of their voices in Dutch.

But it wasn't too bad after all. Neeltje sat her
down, introduced her rapidly and left her to shake
hands all round, while she went to get their meal;
meat balls, a variety of vegetables and a great
many potatoes. Lavinia, who was hungry, ate the
lot, followed it with a bowl of custard, and then,
over coffee, did her best to answer the questions
being put to her. It was an agreeable surprise to

find that most of her companions spoke such good English and were so friendly.

'Are there any other English nurses here?' she wanted to know.

Neeltje shook her head. 'You are the first—there are to be more, but not for some weeks. And now we must go to our work.'

The hospital might be old, but the theatre block was magnificently modern. Lavinia, whisked along by her friendly companion, peered about her and wished that she could tell Peta all about it; she would have to write a letter as soon as possible. But soon, caught up in the familiar routine, she had no time to think about anything or anyone other than her work. It was, as the Directrice had told her, a short list, and the technique was almost exactly the same as it had been in her own hospital, although now and again she was reminded that it wasn't quite the same—the murmur of voices, speaking a strange language, even though everyone there addressed her in English.

Before the list had started, Zuster Smid had introduced her to the surgeon who was taking the list, his registrar and his houseman, as well as the three nurses who were on duty. She had forgotten their names, which was awkward, but at least she knew what she was doing around theatre. Zuster Smid had watched her closely for quite a while and then had relaxed. Lavinia, while not much to look at, was competent at her job; it would take more than working in strange surroundings to make her less than that.

The afternoon came to an end, the theatre was readied once more for the morning's work or any emergency which might be sent up during the night, and shepherded by the other girls, she went down to her supper and after that she was swept along to Neeltje's room with half a dozen other girls, to drink coffee and gossip—she might have been back at Jerrold's. She stifled a sudden pang of homesickness, telling herself that she was tired—as indeed she was, for no sooner had she put her head on her pillow than she was asleep.

It was on her third day, at the end of a busy morning's list, that she was asked to go up to the next floor with a specimen for section. The Path. Lab. usually sent an assistant down to collect these, but this morning, for some reason, there was no one to send and Lavinia, not scrubbed, and nearest to take the receiver with the offending object to be investigated, slid out of the theatre with it, divested herself of her gown and over-shoes and made her way swiftly up the stairs outside the theatre unit.

The Path. Lab. was large—owing, she had been told, to the fact that Professor ter Bavinck, who was the head of it, was justly famed for his brilliant work. Other, smaller hospitals sent a constant stream of work and he was frequently invited to other countries in order to give his learned opinion on some pathological problem. Neeltje had related this in a reverent voice tinged with awe, and Lavinia had concluded that the professor was an object of veneration in the hospital; possibly he had a white beard.

She pushed open the heavy glass doors in front of her and found herself in a vast room, brightly lighted and full of equipment which she knew of, but never quite understood. There were a number of men sitting at their benches, far too busy to take any notice of her, so she walked past them to the end of the room where there was a door with the professor's name on it; presumably this was where one went. But when she knocked, no one answered, so she turned her back on it and looked round the room.

One man drew her attention at once, and he was sitting with his back to her, looking through a microscope. It was the breadth of his shoulders which had caught her eye, and his pale as flax hair, heavily silvered. She wondered who he might be, but now wasn't the time to indulge her interest.

She addressed the room in general in a quite loud voice. 'Professor ter Bavinck? I've been sent from Theatre B with a specimen.'

The shoulders which had caught her eye gave
an impatient shrug; without turning round a deep
voice told her: 'Put it down here, beside me,
please, and then go away.'

Lavinia's charming bosom swelled with indignation. What a way to talk, and who did he think
he was, anyway? She advanced to his desk and laid
the kidney dish silently at his elbow. 'There you
are, sir,' she said with a decided snap, 'and why
on earth should you imagine I should want to
stay?'

He lifted his head then to stare at her, and she
found herself staring back at a remarkably handsome face; a high-bridged nose dominated it and
the mouth beneath it was very firm, while the blue
eyes studying her so intently were heavy-lidded
and heavily browed. She was quite unprepared for
his friendly smile and for the great size of him as
he pushed back his chair and stood up, towering
over her five feet four inches.

'Ah, the English nurse—Miss Hawkins, is it
not? In fact, I am sure,' his smile was still friendly,
'no nurse in the hospital would speak to me like
that.'

Lavinia went a splendid pink and sought for
something suitable to say to this. After a moment's
thought she decided that it was best to say nothing
at all, so she closed her mouth firmly and met his

eyes squarely. Perhaps she had been rude, but after all, he had asked for it. Her uneasy thoughts were interrupted by his voice, quite brisk now. 'This specimen—a snap check, I presume—Mevrouw Vliet, the query mastectomy, isn't it?'

'Yes, sir.'

'I'll telephone down.' He nodded at her in a kindly, uncle-ish way, said: 'Run along,' and turned away, the kidney dish on his hand. She heard him giving what she supposed to be instructions to one of his assistants as she went through the door.

She found herself thinking about him while they all waited for his report; the surgeon, his sterile gloved hands clasped before him, the rest of them ready to do exactly what he wanted when he said so. The message came very quickly. Lavinia wondered what the professor had thought when his sharp eyes had detected the cancer cells in the specimen, but possibly Mevrouw Vliet, lying unconscious on the table and happily unaware of what was happening, was just another case to him. He might not know—nor care—if she were young, old, pretty or plain, married or unmarried, and yet he had looked as though he might—given the right circumstances—be rather super.

It was much later, at supper time, that Neeltje wanted to know what she had thought of him.

'Well,' said Lavinia cautiously, 'I hardly spoke to him—he just took the kidney dish and told me to go away.'

'And that was all?'

'He did remark that I was the English nurse. He's…he's rather large, isn't he?'

'From Friesland,' explained Neeltje, who was from Friesland herself. 'We are a big people. He is of course old.'

Lavinia paused in the conveyance of soup to her mouth. 'Old?' she frowned. 'I didn't think he looked old.'

'He is past forty,' said a small brown-haired girl from across the table. 'Also he has been married; his daughter is fourteen.'

There were a dozen questions on Lavinia's tongue, but it wasn't really her business. All the same, she did want to know what had happened to his wife. The brown-haired girl must have read her thoughts, for she went on: 'His wife died ten years ago, more than that perhaps, she was, how do you say? not a good wife. She was not liked, but the professor, now he is much liked, although he talks to no one, that is to say, he talks but he tells nothing, you understand? Perhaps he is unhappy, but he would not allow anyone to see that and never has he spoken of his wife.' She shrugged. 'Perhaps he loved her, who knows? His daughter is very nice, her name is Sibendina.'

'That's pretty,' said Lavinia, still thinking about the professor. 'Is that a Friesian name?'

'Yes, although it is unusual.' Neeltje swallowed the last of her coffee. 'Let us go to the sitting-room and watch the *televisie*.'

Lavinia met the professor two days later. She had been to her first Dutch lesson in her off duty, arranged for her by someone on the administrative staff and whom probably she would never meet but who had nonetheless given her careful instruction as to her ten-minute walk to reach her teacher's flat. This lady turned out to be a retired school-mistress with stern features and a command of the English language which quite deflated Lavinia. However, at the end of an hour, Juffrouw de Waal was kind enough to say that her pupil, provided she applied herself to her work, should prove to be a satisfactory pupil, worthy of her teaching powers.

Lavinia wandered back in the warmth of the summer afternoon, and with time on her hands, turned off the main street she had been instructed to follow, to stroll down a narrow alley lined with charming little houses. It opened on to a square, lined with trees and old, thin houses leaning against each other for support. They were three or four stories high, with a variety of roofs, and here

and there they had been crowded out by much
larger double-fronted town mansions, with steps
leading up to their imposing doors. She inspected
them all, liking their unassuming façades and trying to guess what they would be like on the other
side of their sober fronts. Probably quite splendid
and magnificently furnished; the curtains, from
what she could see from the pavement, were lav-
ishly draped and of brocade or velvet. She had
completed her walk around three sides of the
square when she was addressed from behind.

'I hardly expected to find you here, Miss Hawkins—not lost, I hope?'

She turned round to confront Professor ter Bavinck. 'No—at least...' She paused to look around
her; she wasn't exactly lost, but now she had no
idea which lane she had come from. 'I've been for
an English lesson,' she explained defensively, 'and
I had some time to spare, and it looked so delightful...' She gave another quick look around her. 'I
only have to walk along that little lane,' she assured him.

He laughed gently. 'No, not that one—the people who live in this square have their garages there
and it's a cul-de-sac. I'm going to the hospital, you
had better come along with me.'

'Oh, no—that is, it's quite all right.' She had
answered very fast, anxious not to be a nuisance

and at the same time aware that this large quiet man had a strange effect upon her.

'You don't like me, Miss Hawkins?'

She gave him a shocked look, and it was on the tip of her tongue to assure him that she was quite sure, if she allowed herself to think about it, that she liked him very much, but all she said was: 'I don't know you, Professor, do I? But I've no reason not to like you. I only said that because you might not want my company.'

'Don't beg the question; we both have our work to do there this afternoon, and that is surely a good enough reason to bear each other company.' He didn't wait to hear her answer. 'We go this way.'

He started to walk back the way she had come, past the tall houses squeezed even narrower and taller by the great house in their centre—it took up at least half of that side of the square, and moreover there was a handsome Bentley convertible standing before its door.

Lavinia slowed down to look at it. 'A Bentley!' she exclaimed, rather superfluously. 'I thought everybody who could afford to do so drove Mercedes on the continent. I wonder whose it is—it must take a good deal of cunning to get through that lane I walked down.'

'This one's wider,' her companion remarked carelessly, and turned into a short, quite broad

street leading away from the square. It ran into
another main street she didn't recognize, crowded
with traffic, but beyond advising her to keep her
eyes and ears open the professor had no conversation. True, when they had to cross the street, he
took her arm and saw her safely to the other side,
but with very much the tolerant air of someone
giving a helping hand to an old lady or a small
child. It was quite a relief when he plunged down
a narrow passage between high brick walls which
ended unexpectedly at the very gates of the hospital.

'Don't try and come that way by yourself,' he
cautioned her, lifted a hand in salute and strode
away across the forecourt. Lavinia went to her
room to change, feeling somehow disappointed, although she wasn't sure why. Perhaps, she told herself, it was because she had been wearing a rather
plain dress; adequate enough for Juffrouw de
Waal, but lacking in eye-catching qualities. Not
that it would have mattered; the professor hadn't
bothered to look at her once—and why should he?
Rather plain girls were just as likely two a penny
in Holland as they were in England. She screwed
her hair into a shining bun, jammed her cap on top
of it, and went on duty, pretending to herself that
she didn't care in the least whether she saw him
again or not.

She saw him just one hour later. There had been an emergency appendix just after she had got back to theatre, and she had been sent back to the ward with the patient. She and one of the ward nurses were tucking the patient into her bed, when she glanced up and saw him, sitting on a nearby bed, listening attentively to its occupant. The ward nurse leaned across the bed. 'Professor ter Bavinck,' she breathed, 'so good a man and so kind— he visits…' she frowned, seeking words. 'Mevrouw Vliet, the mastectomy—you were at the operation and you know what was discovered? When that is so, he visits the patient and explains and listens and helps if he can.' She paused to smile. 'My English—it is not so bad, I hope?'

'It's jolly good. I wish I knew even a few words of Dutch.' Lavinia meant that; it would be nice to understand what the professor was saying—not that she was likely to get much chance of that.

She handed over the patient's notes, and without looking at the professor, went back to theatre. Zuster Smid had gone off duty, taking most of her staff with her, there were only Neeltje and herself working until nine o'clock. She had been sorting instruments while her companion saw to the theatre linen, when the door opened and Professor ter Bavinck walked in. He walked over to say something to Neeltje before he came across the theatre to Lavinia.

'Off at nine o'clock?' he asked.

'Yes, sir.'

His mouth twitched faintly. 'Could you stop calling me sir? Just long enough for me to invite you out to supper.'

'Me? Supper?' Her eyes were round with surprise. 'Oh, but I…'

'Scared of being chatted up? Forget it, dear girl; think of me as a Dutch uncle anxious to make you feel at home in Amsterdam.'

She found herself smiling. 'I don't know what a Dutch uncle is.'

'I'm vague about it myself, but it sounds respectable enough to establish a respectable relationship, don't you agree?'

A warning, perhaps? Letting her know in the nicest way that he was merely taking pity on a stranger who might be feeling lonely?

'Somewhere quiet,' he went on, just as if she had already said that she would go with him, 'where we can get a quick snack—I'll be at the front entrance.'

'I haven't said that I'll go yet,' she reminded him coldly, and wished that she hadn't said it, for the look he bent on her was surprised and baffled too, so that she rushed on: 'I didn't mean that—of course I'll come, I'd like to.'

He didn't smile although his eyes twinkled reassuringly. 'We don't need to be anything but honest with each other,' a remark which left her, in her turn, surprised and baffled. He had gone while she was still thinking it over, and any vague and foolish ideas which it might have nurtured were at once dispelled by Neeltje's, 'You go to supper with the Prof. Did I not tell you how good and kind a man he is? He helps always the lame dog...'

Just for a moment the shine went out of the evening, but Lavinia was blessed with a sense of humour; she giggled and said cheerfully: 'Well, let's hope I get a good supper, because I'm hungry.'

She changed rapidly, not quite sure what she should wear or how much time she had in which to put it on. It was a warm evening and still light; still damp from a shower, she looked over her sketchy wardrobe and decided that the pink cotton with its jacket would look right wherever they went. As she did her face and hair she tried to remember if there were any snack bars or cafés close to the hospital, but with the exception of Jan's Eethuisje just across the road and much frequented by the hospital staff who had had to miss a meal for some reason or other, she could think of none. She thrust her feet into the pink sandals, checked her handbag's contents and made her way to the entrance.

The professor was there; it wasn't until she saw him, leaning against the wall, his hands in his pockets, that she realized that she hadn't been quite sure that he would be. He came across the hall to meet her and she noticed that his clothes were good; elegant and beautifully cut if a little conservative—but then he wasn't a very young man.

He said hullo in a casual way and opened the door for her and they went out to the forecourt together. It was fairly empty, but even if it hadn't been, any cars which might have been there would have been cast into the shade by the car outside the door.

'Oh, it's the Bentley!' cried Lavinia as her companion ushered her into its luxury.

'You like it? I need a large car, you see.' He got in beside her. 'One of the problems of being large.'

She sat back, sniffing the faint scent of leather, enjoying the drive, however short, in such a fabulous car. And the drive was short; the professor slid in and out of the traffic while she was still trying to discover which way they were going, and pulled up after only a few minutes, parking the car on the cobbles at the side of the narrow canal beside an even narrower street, and inviting her to get out. It seemed that their snack was to be taken at what appeared to be an expensive restaurant, its name displayed so discreetly that it could have passed for a town house in a row of similar houses. Lavinia allowed herself to be shepherded inside to a quiet luxury which took her breath and sitting at a table which had obviously been reserved for them, thanked heaven silently that the pink, while not anything out of the ordinary, at least passed muster.

It was equally obvious within a very few moments that the professor's notion of a quick snack wasn't hers. She ran her eyes over the large menu card, looking in vain for hamburgers or baked beans on toast, although she doubted if such an establishment served such homely dishes.

'Smoked eel?' invited her companion. 'I think you must try that, and then perhaps coq au vin to follow?' He dismissed the waiter and turned to confer with the wine waiter, asking as he did so: 'Sherry for you? Do you prefer it sweet?'

She guessed quite rightly that it wasn't likely to be the same sort of sherry they drank at hospital parties. 'Well...' she smiled at him, 'I don't know much about it—would you choose?'

The sherry, when it came, was faintly dry and as soft as velvet. Lavinia took a cautious second sip, aware, that she hadn't had much to eat for some time, aware, too, that conversationally she wasn't giving very good value. Her host was sitting back in his chair, completely at his ease, his eyes on her face, so that she found it difficult to think of something to talk about. She was on the point of falling back on the weather when he said: 'Tell me about yourself—why did you take this job? Did not your family dislike the idea of you coming here? There are surely jobs enough in England for someone as efficient as you.' He saw the look on her face and added: 'Dear me, I did put that badly, didn't I? It just shows you that a lack of female society makes a man very clumsy with his words.'

She took another sip of sherry. 'I haven't a family—at least, only a sister. She's fifteen, almost sixteen, and lives with an aunt. She hasn't been happy with her and when I saw this job advertised I thought I'd try for it—I shall be able to live out, you see, and Peta will be able to come here and live with me. I couldn't do that in England—not in London at any rate, because flats there are very expensive and nurses don't earn an awful lot.'

She finished the sherry. It had loosened her tongue; she hadn't told anyone her plans, and here she was pouring out her heart to a stranger—almost a stranger, then, though he had never seemed to be that, rather someone whom she had known for a very long time.

'You are prepared to take that responsibility?

You should marry.' There was the faintest question in his voice.

'Well, that would be awfully convenient, but no one's asked me, and anyway I can't imagine anyone wanting to make a home for Peta as well as me.'

She couldn't see his eyes very well; the heavy lids almost covered them, probably he was half asleep with boredom. 'I think you may be wrong there,' he said quietly, and then: 'And what do you think of our hospital?'

It was easy after that; he led her from one topic to the next while they ate the smoked eel and then the chicken, washed down with the wine which had been the subject of such serious discussion with the wine waiter. Lavinia had no idea what it was, but it tasted delicious, as did the chocolate mousse which followed the chicken. She ate and drank with the simple pleasure of someone who doesn't go out very often, and when she had finished it, she said shyly: 'That was quite super; I don't go out a great deal—hardly ever, in fact. I thought you meant it when you said a quick snack.'

He laughed gently. 'It's quite some time since I took a girl out to supper. I haven't enjoyed myself so much for a long while.' He added deliberately: 'We must do it again.'

'Yes, well…that would be…' She found herself

short of both breath and words. 'I expect I should be getting back.'

He lifted a finger to the hovering waiter. 'Of course—a heavy day tomorrow, isn't it?'

He spoke very little on their way back to the hospital, and Lavinia, trying to remember it all later, couldn't be sure of what she had replied. He wished her good night at the hospital entrance and got back into his car and drove off without looking back. He was nice, she admitted to herself as she went to her room; the kind of man she felt at ease with—he would be a wonderful friend; perhaps, later on, he might be. She went to sleep thinking about him.

There was the usual chatter at breakfast and several of her table companions asked her if she had had a good supper. Evidently someone had told them. Neeltje probably; she was a positive fount of information about everything and everyone. She informed everyone now: 'The Prof's going to a conference in Vienna; he won't be here for a few days, for I heard him telling Doctor van Teyl about it. We shall have that grumpy old van Vorst snapping our heads off if we have to go to the Path. Lab.' She smiled at Lavinia. 'And he is not likely to ask you to go out with him.'

Everyone laughed and Lavinia laughed too, although in fact she felt quite gloomy. Somehow she had imagined that she would see Professor ter Bavinck again that morning, and the knowledge that she wouldn't seemed to have taken a good deal of the sparkle out of the day.

She settled down during the next few days into her new way of life, writing to Peta every day or so, studying her Dutch lessons hard so that she might wring a reluctant word of praise from Juffrouw de Waal, and when she was on duty, working very hard indeed. She had scrubbed for several cases by now and had managed very well, refusing to allow herself to be distracted or worried by the steady flow of Dutch conversation which went on between the surgeons as they worked, and after all, the instruments were the same, the technique was almost the same, even if they were called by different names. She coped with whatever came her way with her usual unhurried calm.

Only that calm was a little shattered one morning. They were doing a gastro-entreostomy, when the surgeon cast doubts on his findings and sent someone to telephone the Path. Lab. A minute or two later Professor ter Bavinck came in, exchanged a few words with his colleagues, collected the offending piece of tissue which was the cause of the doubt, cast a lightning look at Lavinia, standing behind her trolleys, and went away again.

So he was back. She counted a fresh batch of

swabs, feeling the tide of pleasure the sight of him had engendered inside her. The day had suddenly become splendid and full of exciting possibilities. She only just stopped herself in time from bursting into song.

CHAPTER THREE

BUT THE DAY wasn't splendid at all; she was in theatre for hours as it turned out, with an emergency; some poor soul who had fallen from a fourth floor balcony. The surgeons laboured over her for patient hours and no one thought of going to dinner, although two or three of the nurses managed to get a cup of coffee. But Lavinia, being scrubbed and taking the morning's list, went stoically on until at length, about three o'clock in the afternoon, she had a few minutes in which to bolt a sandwich and drink some coffee, and because the morning's list had been held up it ended hours late; in consequence the afternoon list was late too, and even though she didn't have to scrub, she was still on duty. When she finally got off duty it was well past seven o'clock. There was no reason why she should look for the professor on her way to supper; he was unlikely to be lurking on the stairs or round a corner of any of the maze of passages, so her disappointment at not meeting him was quite absurd. She ate her supper, pleaded tiredness after her long day, and retired to the fastness of her room.

A good night's sleep worked wonders. She felt

quite light-hearted as she dressed the next morning; she would be off at four o'clock and the lists weren't heavy; perhaps she would see Professor ter Bavinck and he would suggest another quick snack... She bounced down to breakfast, not stopping to examine her happiness, only knowing that it was another day and there was the chance of something super happening.

Nothing happened at all. Work, of course—there was always plenty of that; it was a busy hospital and the surgeons who worked there were known for their skill. The morning wore on into the afternoon until it was time for her to go off duty. Neeltje was off too—they were going out with some of the other nurses; a trip round the city's canals was a must for every visitor to Amsterdam and they would take her that very evening. She got ready for the outing, determined to enjoy herself. She had been silly and made too much of the professor's kindness—it was because she went out so seldom with a man that she had attached so much importance to seeing him again. Heaven forbid that she should appear over-eager, indeed, if he were to ask her out again she would take care to have an excuse ready, she told herself stoutly. She stared at her reflection in the looking glass—he wasn't likely to ask her again, anyway. He was in the hospital each day, she had heard someone say so, and there had been plenty of opportunities...

She left her room and took the short cut to the hospital entrance where she was to meet the others. The last few yards of it gave her an excellent view of the forecourt so that she couldn't fail to see the professor standing in it, talking earnestly to a young woman. It was too far off to see if she was pretty, but even at that distance Lavinia could see that she was beautifully dressed. She slowed her steps the better to look and then stopped altogether as he took the girl's arm and walked away with her, across the tarmac to where his motorcar was standing. She didn't move until they had both got into it and it had disappeared through the gates, and when she did she walked very briskly, with her determined little chin rather higher than usual and two bright spots of colour on her cheeks.

When they all got back a couple of hours later, the professor was standing in the entrance, talking to two of the consultants, and all three men wished the girls *Goeden avond*. Lavinia, joining in the polite chorus of replies, took care not to look at him.

She wakened the next morning to remember that it was her day off. The fine weather still held and she had a formidable list of museums to visit. She was up and out soon after nine o'clock, clad in a cool cotton dress and sandals on her bare feet and just enough money in her handbag to pay for her lunch.

She went first to the Bijenkorf, however, that mecca of the Amsterdam shopper, and spent an hour browsing round its departments, wishing she had the money to buy the pretty things on display, cheering herself with the thought that before very long, she might be able to do so. But it was already ten o'clock and the museums had been open half an hour already, she started to walk across the Dam Square, with its palace on one side and the stark war memorial facing it on the other, down Kalverstraat, not stopping to look in the tempting shop windows, and into Leidsestraat. It was here that she noticed that the blue sky had dimmed to grey, it was going to rain—but the museum was only a few minutes' brisk walk away now, she could actually see the imposing frontage of her goal. The first few drops began to fall seconds later, however, and then without warning, turned into a downpour. Lavinia began to run, feeling the rain soaking her thin dress.

The Bentley pulled into the curb a little ahead of her, so that by the time she was level with it the professor was on the pavement, standing in the rain too. He didn't speak at all, merely plucked her neatly from the pavement, bustled her round the elegant bonnet of the car, and popped her into the front seat. When he got in beside her, all he said was: 'You're very wet,' as he drove on.

Lavinia got her breath. 'I was going to the museum,' she began. 'It's only just across the road,' she added helpfully, in case he wanted an excuse to drop her off somewhere quickly.

'Unmistakable, isn't it?' he observed dryly, and drove past it to join the stream of traffic going back into the city's heart.

Her voice came out small. 'Are you taking me back to St Jorus?'

'Good lord, no—on your day off? We're going to get you dry, you can't possibly drip all over the Rijksmuseum.'

He was threading the big car up and down narrow streets which held very little traffic, and she had no idea where she was; she didn't really care, it was nice just to sit there without question. But presently she recognized her surroundings—this was the square she had visited that afternoon, and she made haste to tell him so. 'I remember the houses,' she told him, 'they've got such plain faces, but I'm sure they must be beautiful inside. If you want to set me down here, I know my way—I expect you're going to the hospital.'

'No, I'm not.' He circled the square and on its third side stopped before the large house in the middle of the row of tall, narrower ones, and when she gave him a questioning look, said blandly: 'I live here. My housekeeper will dry that dress of yours for you—and anything else that's wet.' He spoke with friendly casualness. 'We can have our coffee while she's doing it.'

'Very kind,' she said, breathless, 'but your work—I've delayed you already.'

He leaned across her and opened the door before getting out of the car. 'I have an occasional day off myself.' He came round the car and stood by the door while she got out too, and then led her across the narrow cobbled street to his front door.

She had no idea that a house could be so beautiful; true, she had seen pictures of such places in magazines, and she was aware that there were such places, but looking at them in a magazine and actually standing in the real thing were two quite different things. She breathed an ecstatic sigh as she gazed around her; this was better than anything pictured—a large, light hall with an Anatolian carpet in rich reds and blues almost covering its black and white marble floor, with a staircase rising from its end wall, richly carved, its oak treads uncarpeted and a chandelier of vast proportions hanging from a ceiling so high that she had to stretch her neck to see it properly.

'You don't live here?' she wanted to know of her companion, and he gave a short laugh. 'Oh,

but I do—have done all my life. Come along, we'll
find Mevrouw Pette.'

He urged her across the floor to a door at the
back of the hall, beside the staircase and opened it
for her, shouting down the short flight of stairs on
the other side as they began to descend them. At
the bottom there was a narrow door, so low that
he was forced to bow his head to go through. It
gave on to a surprisingly large and cheerful room,
obviously the kitchen, decided Lavinia, trying not
to look too curiously at everything around her.
Nice and old-fashioned, but with all the modern
gadgets any woman could wish for. There were
cheerful yellow curtains at the windows, which
looked out on to a narrow strip of garden at the
back of the house, and the furniture was solid; an
enormous wooden dresser against one wall, a
scrubbed table, equally enormous, in the centre of
the brick floor and tall Windsor chairs on either
side of the Aga cooker. There were cheerful rugs
too, and rows of copper pots and pans on the walls.
It was all very cosy and one hardly noticed the
fridge, the rotisserie and the up-to-date electric
oven tucked away so discreetly. Out of sight, she
felt sure, there would be a washing-up machine and
a deep-freeze and anything else which would make
life easier. The professor must have a very good
job indeed to be able to live so splendidly—and

there were no fewer than three persons working in the kitchen, too. The elderly woman coming to meet them would be the housekeeper and as well as her there was a young girl cleaning vegetables at the sink, while another girl stood at the table clearing away some cooking utensils.

The professor spoke to them as he went in and they looked up and smiled and then went on with what they were doing while he talked to Mevrouw Pette at some length. She was a thin woman, of middle height, with a sharp nose and a rosy complexion, her hair, still a nice brown, drawn back severely from her face. But she had a kind smile; she smiled at Lavinia now and beckoned to her, and encouraged by the professor's: 'Yes, go along, Lavinia—Mevrouw Pette will take your dress and lend you a dressing gown and bring you down again for coffee,' Lavinia followed.

So she went back up the little stair once more and across the hall to the much grander staircase and mounted it in Mevrouw Pette's wake, to be ushered into a dear little room, all chintz and dark oak, where she took off her dress and put on the dressing gown the housekeeper produced. It was blue satin, quilted and expensive; she wondered whose it was—surely not Mevrouw Pette's? It fitted tolerably well, though she was just a little plump for it. She smoothed back her damp hair, frowned at herself in the great mirror over the oak dower chest against one wall, and was escorted downstairs once more, this time to a room on the right of the hall—a very handsome room, although having seen a little of the house, she wasn't surprised at that. All the same, she had to admit that its rich comfort, allied with beautiful furniture and hangings of a deep sapphire blue, was quite breathtaking.

The professor was standing with his back to the door looking out of a window, but when he turned round she plunged at once into talk, feeling shy. 'You're very kind, and I am sorry to give you so much trouble.'

He waved her to an outsize chair which swallowed her in its vast comfort and sat down himself opposite her. 'I'm a selfish man,' he observed blandly. 'If I hadn't wished to trouble myself, I shouldn't have done so.' He crossed one long leg over the other, very much at his ease. 'You didn't look at me yesterday evening,' he observed. 'You were annoyed, I think—I hope...and that pleased me, because it meant that you were a little interested in me.'

He smiled at her look of outrage. 'No, don't be cross—did I not say that we could be nothing but honest with each other, as friends should be? I have been back for three days and I had made up my mind not to see you for a little while, and then yesterday I changed my mind, but I met an old friend who needed advice, so I was hindered from asking you to come out with me.'

She had no idea why he was telling her all this, but she had to match his frankness. 'I saw her with you.'

He smiled again. 'Ah, so you were hoping that I would come?'

The conversation was getting out of hand; she said with dignity and a sad lack of truth: 'I didn't hope anything of the sort, Professor,' and was saved from further fibbing by Mevrouw Pette's entrance with the coffee tray, but once the coffee was poured, her relief was short-lived.

'You probably think that I am a conceited middle-aged man who should know better,' said the professor suavely.

She nibbled at a spicy biscuit before she replied. 'No. You're not middle-aged or conceited. And I did hope you'd ask me out again, though I can't think why, me being me. If I were a raving beauty I don't suppose I'd be in the least surprised...'

He laughed then, suddenly years younger. 'Is your young sister like you?' he wanted to know.

'To look at? No; she's pretty, but we like the same things and we get on well together—but then she's easy to get on with.'

'And you are not?'

'I don't know. My aunt says I'm not, but then she doesn't like me, but she has given Peta a home for a year now and sent her to school...'

'But not loved her?'

'No.'

He passed his cup for more coffee. 'You think your sister will like Amsterdam?'

'I'm sure she will. She takes her O levels this week and then she'll leave school—just as soon as I can get somewhere to live here she can come. I thought she could have Dutch lessons...'

'And you plan to stay here for the foreseeable future?'

Lavinia nodded cheerfully, happy to be talking to him. 'I like it, living here. I feel quite at home and I earn so much more, you see, and if I stay here for a year or two I could save some money, enough to go back to England if Peta wanted to, and start her on whatever she decides to do.'

'No plans for yourself?'

She said a little stiffly: 'I'm quite happy, Professor.'

His thick eyebrows arched. 'Yes? I ask too many questions, don't I?' He got up and went to open the french window and a small hairy dog, all tail and large paws, came romping in, followed by an Irish setter, walking with dignity. 'You don't object to dogs?' asked the professor. 'Dong and Pobble like to be with me as much as possible when I'm home.'

Lavinia was on her knees making friends. 'Nonsense Songs!' she cried happily. 'Which one's Dong?'

'The setter. My daughter named them—most people look at me as though I'm mad when I mention their names, but then the Nonsense Songs aren't read very widely.'

'No—my father used to read them to me when I was a little girl.' She got to her feet. 'I'm sure my dress must be dry by now—you've been very kind, but I'm wasting your morning; I'll go and find your housekeeper if I may.'

For answer he tugged the beautifully embroidered bell-pull beside his chair, and when Mevrouw Pette came said something or other which caused her to smile and nod and beckon to Lavinia, who got up obediently and followed her out of the room.

Her dress was dry once more and moreover pressed by an expert hand. She did her face and hair, laid the dressing gown lovingly on the thick silk bed quilt, and went downstairs. The professor was in the hall, and she stifled a pang of disappointment that he appeared so anxious to speed her on her way, even as she achieved a bright, friendly smile and hurried to the door. He opened it as she reached his side and she thrust out a hand, searching frantically for something suitable to say by way of farewell. But there was no need to say anything; he took her hand, but instead of shaking it, he gripped it firmly, whistled piercingly to the dogs, and went out of the door with her. At the car she halted. 'Thank you,' she tried again, in what she hoped was a final sort of voice. 'There's really no need...I know where I am.' She glanced up at the sky, the greyness had changed back to blue once more. 'I shall enjoy walking.'

'Fiddle,' declared her companion, and opened the car door. 'I'm going to show you the Rijksmuseum, and we'll have to take the car because these two like to sit in the back and guard it when I'm not there.'

He opened the other door as he spoke and the two astute animals rushed past him and took up position with a determination which brooked no interference on Lavinia's part; she got in too, at a loss for words.

Her companion didn't appear to notice her silence but drove off with the air of a well-contented man, and only when they were almost at the museum did he remark: 'Everyone comes to see the Nachwacht, of course—it's a wonderful painting, but there are several which I like much better. I'd like to show them to you.' He paused and added gently: 'And if you say how kind just once more, I shall wring your neck!'

Lavinia jumped and gave him a startled look; he wasn't behaving like a professor at all, nor, for that matter, like a man who would never see forty again. 'I can't think why you should speak to me like that,' she reproved him austerely, and was reduced to silence by his: 'Am I cutting the corners too fine for you? It seemed to me that since we liked each other on sight, it would be a little silly to go through all the preliminaries, but if you would prefer that, I'll call you Miss Hawkins for a week or two, erase from my mind the sight of you in Sibendina's dressing gown, and drop you off at the next bus stop.'

She had cried: 'Oh, don't do that,' before she could stop herself, and went on a little wildly: 'You see, I'm not used to—to…well, I don't get asked out much and so none of this seems quite real—more like a dream.'

'But dreams are true while they last—your Tennyson said so, what's more doesn't he go on to say: "And do we not live in dreams?" So no more nonsense, Lavinia.'

He swept the car into the great forecourt of the museum, gave the dogs a quiet command and opened her door. He took her arm as they went in together and it seemed the most natural thing in the world that he should do so. She smiled up at him as they paused before the first picture.

There was no hurry. They strolled from one room to the next, to come finally to the enormous Nachtwacht and sit before it for a little while, picking out the figures which peopled the vast canvas, until the professor said: 'Now come and see my favourites.' Two small portraits, an old man and an old woman, wrinkled and blue-eyed and dignified, and so alive that Lavinia felt that she could have held a conversation with them.

'Nice, aren't they?' observed her companion. 'Come and look at the Lelys.'

She liked these even better; she went from one exquisitely painted portrait to the next and back again. 'Look at those pearls,' she begged him. 'They look absolutely real...'

'Well, most likely they were,' he pointed out reasonably. 'Do you like pearls?'

'Me? Yes, of course I do, though I'm not sure that I've ever seen any real ones. The Queen has some, but I don't suppose there are many women who possess any.'

He smiled and she wondered why he looked amused. 'Probably not. Will you have lunch with me, Lavinia?'

She hesitated. 'How k...' She caught the gleam

in his eye then and chuckled delightfully. 'I've never fancied having my neck wrung in public, so I'll say yes, thank you.'

'Wise girl.' He tucked an arm in hers and began to walk to the exit, then stopped to look at her. 'How old are you?' he wanted to know.

She breathed an indignant: 'Well...' then told him: 'Twenty-six,' adding with an engaging twinkle: 'How rude of you to ask!'

'But you didn't mind telling me. I'm getting on for forty-one.'

'Yes, I know.' And at his sharp glance of inquiry: 'One of the nurses told me—not gossiping.'

He said very evenly: 'And you were also told that I am a widower, and that I have a daughter.'

'Oh, yes. You see, they all like you very much— they're a bit scared of you too, I think, but they like it that way—you're a bit larger than life, you know.'

He didn't answer at once, in fact he didn't speak at all during their short drive back to the house, only as he drew up before his door he said in a quiet voice: 'I don't care for flattery, Lavinia.'

Her pleasant face went slowly pink; a quite unaccountable rage shook her. She said on a heaving breath: 'You think that's what I'm doing? Toadying to you? Just because you're smashing to look at and a professor and—and took me out to sup-

per...and so now I'm angling for another meal, am
I?'

She choked on temper while she made furious
efforts to get the car door open. Without success
at first and when she did manage it, his hand came
down on hers and held it fast. His voice was still
quiet, but now it held warmth. 'I don't know why
I said that, Lavinia, unless it was because I wanted
to hear you say that I was wrong—and you have.
No, leave the door alone. I'm sorry—will you forgive me?' And when she didn't answer: 'Lavinia?'

She said stiffly: 'Very well,' and forgot to be
stiff. 'Oh, of course I will; I fly off the handle
myself sometimes—only you sounded horrid.'

'I am quite often horrid—ask my daughter.' His
hand was still on hers, but now he took it away
and opened the door for her, and when she looked
at him he smiled and said: 'Mevrouw Pette has
promised us one of her special lunches, shall we
go in?'

She smiled back; it was all right, they were back
where they had been; a pleasant, easy-going friendship which made her forget that she wasn't a raving beauty, and allowed her to be her own uncomplicated self.

'Super, I'm famished, though I keep meaning
not to eat, you know—only I get hungry.'

He was letting the dogs out and turned round to ask: 'Not eating? A self-imposed penance?'

'No—I'm trying to get really slim.'

Dong and Pobble were prancing round her and she bent to rub their ears and then jumped at his sudden roar. 'You just go on eating,' he said forcefully. 'I like to be able to tell the front of a woman from her back, these skeletal types teetering round on four-inch soles don't appeal to me.'

She laughed. 'It would take months of dieting to get me to that state, but I promise you I'll eat a good lunch, just to please you.'

They went into the house then, the dogs racing ahead once they were inside so that they could sit as near the professor as possible, while Lavinia went upstairs to do things to her face and hair, and when she came down again they had drinks, talking companionably, before going into lunch, laid in what the professor called the little sitting-room, which turned out to be almost as large as the room they had just come from.

'The dining-room is so vast that we feel lost in it,' he explained, and then as a door banged: 'Ah, here is Sibendina.'

Lavinia had only just noticed that there were places laid for three on the table and she wasn't sure if she was pleased or not; she was curious to meet the professor's daughter, but on the other hand she had been looking forward to being alone with him. She turned to look over her shoulder as the girl came into the room, at the same time advising herself not to become too interested in the professor and his family; he had befriended her out of kindness and she must remember that.

Sibendina was like her father, tall and big and fair, with his blue eyes but fortunately with someone else's nose, for his, while exactly right on his own handsome face, would have looked quite overpowering on her pretty one. She came across the room at a run, embraced her father with pleasure and then looked at Lavinia, and when he had introduced them with easy good manners, she shook hands, exclaiming: 'I've heard about you—may I call you Lavinia? I've been looking forward to meeting you.'

She sat down opposite her father and grinned engagingly. 'Now I can practise my English,' she declared.

'Why not, Sibby? Although Lavinia might like to practise her Dutch—she's already having lessons.'

'And hours of homework,' said Lavinia, 'which I feel compelled to do, otherwise Juffrouw de Waal makes me feel utterly worthless.'

They all laughed as Mevrouw Pette brought in lunch, and presently the talk was of everything under the sun, with Sibendina asking a great many questions about England and Peta's school. 'She isn't much older than I am,' she observed, 'but she sounds very clever—what is she going to study next?'

'Well, I don't really know; if she comes here to live with me I thought she might have Dutch lessons, then if she's passed her eight O levels, she might be able to take a secretarial course—the Common Market,' Lavinia finished a little vaguely.

'Not nursing?' the professor wanted to know.

Lavinia shook her head. 'Peta's too gentle—she can't stand people being angry or bad-tempered, and there's quite a bit of that when you start training.'

Sibendina was peeling a peach. 'She sounds nice, I should like very much to meet her. When does she come?'

'I don't know if the hospital will keep me yet—if it's OK I'll find somewhere to live and then go and fetch her.'

'And this aunt she lives with—will she not mind?'

Lavinia smiled at the girl. 'I think perhaps she will mind very much—I'm rather dreading it, but I promised Peta.'

'But if you did not go what would your sister do?'

'I think she might run away,' said Lavinia soberly. 'You see, she's not very happy.'

Sibendina looked at the professor, sitting quietly and saying almost nothing. 'Papa, you must do something.' She looked at the Friesian wall clock. 'I have to go; I shall be late for class—you will excuse me, please.' She went round the table and kissed her father. 'Papa,' she said persuasively, 'you will do something, please. I like Lavinia very much and I think that I shall like Peta too.'

He spoke to her but he looked at Lavinia. 'Well, that's a good thing,' he observed blandly, 'for I'm going to ask Lavinia to marry me—not at once, I shall have to wait for her to get used to the idea.'

Lavinia felt the colour leave her face and then come rushing back into it. She hardly heard Sibendina's crow of delighted laughter as she ran out of the room, calling something in Dutch as she went. She was looking at the professor who, in his turn, was watching her closely. 'Don't look like that,' he said in a matter-of-fact voice. 'I shan't do anything earth-shattering like dropping on one knee and begging for your hand; just let the idea filter through, and we'll bring the matter up again in a few days. In the meantime what about a brisk walk to the Dam Palace? It's open for inspection and worth a visit.'

She spoke in a voice which was almost a whisper. 'Yes, that would be very nice—I've always wanted to see inside a palace. Is it far?'

'No, but we'll go the long way round; the nicest part of Amsterdam is tucked away behind the main streets.'

She could see that he had meant what he had said; he wasn't going to do anything earth-shattering. With an effort she forced herself back on to the friendly footing they had been on before he had made his amazing remark, and even discussed with some degree of intelligence the architecture of the old houses they passed, and once they had reached the palace, her interest in it and its contents became almost feverish in her efforts to forget what he had said.

They had tea at Dikker and Thijs and then walked slowly down Kalverstraat while she looked in the shop windows; a pleasant, normal occupation which soothed her jumping nerves, as did her companion's gentle flow of nothings, none of which needed much in the way of replies on her part. They turned away from the shops at last and the professor led her through the narrow streets without telling her where they were going, so that when they rounded a corner and there was the hospital a stone's throw away, Lavinia almost choked with disappointment. He was going to say good-bye; he had decided to deliver her back safely after a pleasant day, foisted on him by the accident of the rain. He had been joking, she told herself savagely—he and Sibendina, and she had actually been taken in. She swallowed the great unmanageable lump in her throat and said politely: 'Well, good-bye—it's been lovely...'

His surprise was genuine. 'What on earth are you talking about? I've only brought you back so that you can change your dress—we're going out to dinner.'

She didn't stop the flood of delight which must have shown in her face. 'Oh, are we? I didn't know.'

He shepherded her across the street and in through the hospital gates. 'I'll be here at seven o'clock, Lavinia—and don't try and do any deep thinking—just make yourself pretty and be ready for me.'

Her, 'Yes, all right,' was very meek.

CHAPTER FOUR

LAVINIA HADN'T brought many clothes with her; she hadn't much of a wardrobe anyway. She searched through her cupboard now and came to the conclusion that it would have to be the green silk jersey, with its tucked bodice gathered into a wide band which emphasized her small waist and its full sleeves, deeply cuffed; it wasn't exactly spectacular, but it would pass muster. All the same, as she put it on, she wished fervently that it had been a Gina Franati model; something quite super to match the professor's faultlessly tailored clothes.

Anxious not to be late, she hurried down to the entrance to find him already there, deep in conversation with one of the doctors, and at the sight of his elegance she regretted, once again, the paucity of her wardrobe. But there was no point in brooding over that now. She hitched her coat over one arm and when he turned and saw her, went to meet him, and the pleased look he gave her quite compensated her for having to wear the green jersey. It was flattering too, the way he took her arm and included her in the conversation he was having for a few minutes. She liked him for that; his man-

ners were beautiful, even if he did startle her sometimes with the things he said.

As they got into the Bentley he said: 'I thought
we might drive over to den Haag, it's only thirty
miles or so. We'll go on the motorway; it's dull,
I'm afraid, but I've booked a table for eight
o'clock.'

She had expected to feel a little awkward with
him, but she didn't. They talked about all manner
of things, but not about themselves; she still wasn't
sure if he had been joking with Sibendina, and
there was no way of finding out, only by asking
him, and that she would never do. She would have
to wait and see; in the meantime she was going to
enjoy herself.

And she did. They dined at the Saur restaurant
in the heart of den Haag—upstairs, in a formal,
almost Edwardian room, and the food was delicious. She wanted the evening to go on for ever;
she knew by now that she liked the professor very
much, although she wasn't going to admit to any
deeper feelings, not until she knew the truth about
his astonishing remark about marrying her. She
didn't know much about falling in love, but she
suspected that this was what was happening to her,
but presumably it was something one could check
or even smother before it became too strong.

They walked about the town after they had

dined, and the professor pointed out the Ridder-
zaal, the Mauritshuis museum, some of the more
interesting statues, an ancient prison gate and the
old City Hall, and then strolled goodnaturedly beside her while she took a brief peep at the tempting
displays in the shop windows.

On the way back to Amsterdam, tearing along
the motorway, they didn't talk a great deal and
then only of trifling things, but as they neared the
hospital the professor said: 'I have to work tomorrow—a pity, I should have enjoyed taking you for
a run in the car. We could have had a swim.'

Lavinia made a mental note to buy a swimsuit
first thing in the morning. 'I've a whole lot of museums to see,' she told him brightly.

'Yes? May I pick you up tomorrow evening?
Seven o'clock?'

She watched his large capable hands on the
wheel and felt her heart tumbling around inside
her. 'I'd like that very much,' she said in a sedate
voice.

At the hospital entrance he got out to open her
door and walk with her across the forecourt to the
farther side where a covered way led to the nurses'
home. His good night was pleasant and formal.

Lavinia went to bed, her head filled with a mud-
dle of thoughts; the pleasant and the not so pleasant

jostling each other for a place until she fell into an uneasy sleep.

She was pottering along the corridor to make herself some tea the next morning when she met Neeltje and several other nurses going down to breakfast. They were almost late, but that didn't prevent them from stopping to greet her and then break into a babble of questions. It was Neeltje who said in her own peculiar brand of English: 'We hear all—Becke Groeneveld sees you with Professor ter Bavinck as you return—that is for the second time that you go out with him. We are all most curious and excited.'

The ring of cheerful faces around her wore pleased smiles, rather as though their owners had engineered her outing amongst themselves. She was touched by their interest and their complete lack of envy; the least she could do was to tell them about her day—well, at least parts of it. 'Well, you see,' she began, 'I got caught in the rain and the professor happened to be passing in his car, so he took me to his house and his housekeeper dried my dress.'

Her listeners regarded her with motherly expressions. 'Well?' they chorused.

'We went to the Rijksmuseum after lunch—oh, and I met his daughter, she's a sweet girl.' The memory of the professor's conversation with Sibendina was suddenly vivid in her mind and she went rather pink. 'I—we, that is, went to dinner in the Hague.'

'You and the Prof?'

She nodded.

'And you go again?' asked Neeltje.

'Well, as a matter of fact, yes.'

'We are glad,' declared Neeltje, 'we have pleasure in this, you understand. But now we must hurry or we do not eat.'

They cried their *tot ziens* and tumbled down the stairs, laughing and talking, and Lavinia made her tea and got dressed slowly, trying not to think about the professor. But it wasn't easy, and later in the morning, even in the most interesting museums, his face kept getting between her and the exhibits she examined so carefully. She had her coffee and then, satisfied with her morning's sightseeing, went to the Bijenkorf and had a snack lunch, then went to look in the shop windows again, making a mental and ever-lengthening list of things she would buy when she had some money. And always at the back of her mind was the professor. By five o'clock she decided that she might well return to the hospital and get ready for her evening, and it was only with the greatest difficulty that she stopped herself from tearing back as though she had a train to catch. She told herself to stop behaving like a fool and forced her feet to a slow pace, so that she was in a fine state of nervous tension by the time she reached the hospital. She went at once to the home and looked at the letter board; there might be a letter from Peta. There was. There was another one, too, in a scrawled handwriting which she knew at once was the professor's. She tore it open and read the one line written on the back of a Path. Lab. form. It stated simply: 'Sorry, can't make it this evening,' and was signed M. ter B. She folded it carefully and put it back in its envelope, then took it out again and re-read it with the air of someone who hoped for a miracle, but there it was, in black and white.

She went slowly to her room, put the note in her handbag and kicked off her sandals. Her disappointment was engulfing her in great waves, but she refused to give way to it; she sat down and opened Peta's letter and started to read it. It was lengthy and unhappy too; Aunt Gwyneth, it seemed, was taking every opportunity to remind Peta that she depended entirely upon her charity and had made veiled hints as to what might happen should Peta fail to get her O levels. Ungrateful girls who didn't work hard enough for exams could not be expected to live in the lap of luxury for ever; there were jobs for them, simple jobs which required no advanced education costing a great deal of money, her aunt had said—a great girl of sixteen would do very well as a companion to some elderly lady…

Lavinia, noting the carefully wiped away tear stains, longed for just half an hour with her sister, but although that wasn't possible, a letter was. She sat down and wrote it, then and there, filling it full of heartening ideas, painting a cheerful picture of the life they would lead together, and that not so far off now. She went out to post it and then went to supper, where she parried her new friends' anxious questions as cheerfully as she could. It was when Neeltje joined them that she discovered where the professor had gone: Utrecht, to some urgent consultation or other. The news cheered her a little. It wasn't until that moment that she admitted to herself that she had been imagining him spending the evening with some fascinating and exquisitely dressed beauty.

Theatre was busy the following day and Lavinia scrubbed for the afternoon list. They were half way through a splenectomy when the professor came in; he was in theatre kit, and after a nod in the general direction of those scattered around, took his place by the surgeon who was operating. He stayed for five minutes or so, peering down at the work being done while he and his colleague muttered together. Finally, he took the offending organ away with him. Lavinia had the impression that he hadn't seen her.

She felt even more certain of this by the time she went off duty at five o'clock, for she had seen him with her own eyes, leaving the forecourt; she had glanced idly out of an upstairs window and then stayed to watch him drive the Bentley out of the gates—out of sight.

Some of the nurses had asked her to go to the cinema with them, but she had pleaded letters to write, aware that if the professor should ask her to go out with him the letters would get short shrift, but now it looked as though that was the way she was going to spend her evening. She showered and changed into slacks and a cotton blouse and made herself some coffee, having no wish for her supper, and then started on her writing; it wasn't very successful, probably because her mind wasn't on it; she gave up after the second letter and went down to the post, thinking, as she went through the hospital, that she would ask to see the Directrice in the morning about living out; perhaps if her future plans were settled she might feel more settled herself. She was turning away from the post box in the front hall when she came face to face with the professor. Her first reaction was sheer delight at seeing him, the second one of annoyance because she must surely look a fright, consequently her 'Good evening, Professor,' was distant, but he ignored that.

'I was on my way over to see you,' he said cheerfully. 'I thought we might spend the evening together.'

A medley of strong feelings left her speechless. Presently she managed: 'I hadn't planned to go out this evening.'

His answer infuriated her. 'Well, I didn't expect you would have—just in case I came...' He gave her an interested look. 'Are you sulking?'

'I have no reason to sulk.'

'Oh? I thought you might because I had to cancel our date yesterday.' He grinned. 'I did think of mentioning it in theatre this afternoon, but I didn't think you would like that.'

She drew a deep breath. 'Professor...' she began, and was cut short by his bland: 'My dear girl, how is our relationship going to progress if you insist on calling me professor at every other breath? My name's Radmer.'

'Oh, is it? I've never heard it before.'

'Naturally not; it's a Friesian name, and you're English.' He smiled with great charm. 'Shall we go?'

'Like this? I'm not dressed for going out.'

He studied her deliberately. 'You're decently

covered,' he observed at length. 'I like your hair hanging down your back. If it will make you happier, we're only going home for dinner—just two friends sharing a meal,' he added matter-of-factly.

'Well, all right.' She gave in with a composure which quite concealed her indignation. No girl, however inadequately dressed, likes to be told that she's decently covered—not in that casual, don't care voice. She got into the Bentley with an hauteur which brought a little smile to her companion's mouth, although he said nothing. But he did set himself out to entertain her over dinner, and his apologies for breaking their date the previous evening were all that any girl could wish for; her good nature reasserted itself and she felt happier than she had felt all day. His undemanding small talk, allied to the smoked salmon, duckling with orange sauce, and fresh fruit salad with its accompanying whipped cream and served on exquisite china, all combined to act on her stretched nerves like balm. She found herself telling him about Peta's letter and what she intended doing about it.

He listened gravely, watching her across the table. When she had finished he observed: 'I see— well, Lavinia, I said that you should have time, did I not, but now I think that we must settle the matter here and now.' He smiled at her with faint mockery. 'Any maidenly ideas you may have been cherishing about being courted, wooed and won must go by the board.'

She sat up very straight in her chair. 'You're not serious?'

'Indeed I am. If you have finished, shall we go to the sitting-room for coffee? Sibby is out with friends and we shall be undisturbed.'

Coffee seemed a good idea, if only to clear her head and dispel the somewhat reckless mood the excellent wine they had had engendered.

She poured it from a charming little silver coffee pot into delicate Sèvres china and wished that her companion wouldn't stare quite so hard at her; she concluded that it was because he was waiting for her to say something, so she asked composedly: 'Would you mind explaining?'

'It's very simple, Lavinia. I have no wife, and a daughter who badly needs female company—to designate you as stepmother would be absurd, but a kind of elder sister? And there is Peta, just a little older than Sibby and an ideal companion for her...'

'They might hate each other.'

He shook his head. 'No, Sibby is likely to take to her on sight; remember that she already likes you very much. And then there is me; I need some-one to entertain for me, buy Sibby's clothes, run my home, and I hope, be my companion.' He was silent for a moment. 'I am sometimes lonely, Lavinia.'

He got up and came and stood in front of her and pulled her to her feet, and put his hands on her shoulders. 'There is no question of falling in love, my dear. I think I may never do that again—once bitten, twice shy—as you say in English. Ours would be a marriage of friends, you understand, no more than that. But I promise you that I will take care of you and Peta, just as I shall take care of Sibby.'

Lavinia swallowed. 'Why me?' she asked in a small voice.

He smiled a little. 'You're sensible, your feet are firmly planted on the ground and you haven't been too happy, have you? You will never be tempted to reach for the moon, my dear.'

She was speechless once more. So that was what he thought of her—a rather dreary spinster type with no ambition to set the world on fire. How wrong he was, and yet in a way, how right. If she chose to refuse his strange offer, the future didn't hold very much for her, she knew that. Several more years of getting Peta on to her own feet and then, when her sister married, as she most certainly would, she herself would be left to a bachelor girl's existence. But to marry this man who was so certain that his idea was a good one? She was old-fashioned enough—and perhaps sentimental enough too—to believe in falling in love and marrying for that reason.

'Would it be honest—I mean, marrying you? I've very little to offer. Sibendina might grow to dislike me, you know, and I'm not much good at entertaining or running a large house.'

'If I tell you that I'm quite sure that it will be a success, will you consider it?'

It was a crazy conversation; she said so and he laughed in genuine amusement. 'Will you think about it, Lavinia?'

'Well—yes.' Even as she said it, she marvelled at herself; her usually sensible head was filled with a mass of nonsense which, once she was alone, she would have to reduce to proper proportions. Indeed, it had suddenly become an urgent matter to get away from this large man who so disquieted her, and think coolly about everything, without his eyes watching her face as though he could read every thought. She said abruptly: 'Would you mind very much if I went back now? I have to think.'

He made no attempt to dissuade her; in no time at all she found herself running up the Home stairs, his brief, friendly good night echoing in her ears.

Being alone didn't help at all, she found herself wishing that he was there so that she might ask his advice, which, on the face of it, was just too absurd. Not only that, her thoughts didn't make sense. Probably she was too tired to think clearly, she would go to bed and sleep, and in the morning she would be able to come to a rational decision.

Amazingly, she slept almost as soon as her head touched the pillow, to waken in time to hear the carillons from Amsterdam's many churches ringing out three o'clock. She buried her head in the pillow, willing herself to go to sleep again. There was a busy day ahead of her in theatre, and in another three hours or so she would have to get up. But her mind, nicely refreshed, refused to do her bidding. 'Radmer,' she said aloud to the dark room. 'It's a strange name, but it suits him.' She turned over in bed and thumped her pillows; somehow it helped to talk to herself about him. 'I wish I knew more about his wife. Perhaps he loved her very much, even if no one else seems to have liked her.'

What was it he had said? Once bitten, twice shy. Anyway, he had made it very plain that he wasn't marrying her because he loved her, only because he liked her.

Lavinia gave up the idea of sleep, and sat up in bed, hugging her knees. She didn't know him at all, really, and it was preposterous that after such a short acquaintance, he should wish to marry her. Primarily for his own convenience, of course, he had made no bones about that; someone to look after Sibby and order his household and entertain for him, he had said; just as though she had no feelings in the matter. She was suddenly indignant and just as suddenly sleepy. When she woke, the sun was up and she could hear the maid coming along the passage, knocking on the doors.

By the time she had dressed she had made up her mind not to marry him, although this decision depressed her dreadfully, and that very day she would see the Directrice and arrange about living out; that would make an end of the matter. She sat silently through breakfast so that Neeltje wanted to know if she felt ill. She made some remark about seeing too many museums all at once and everyone laughed as they dispersed to their various wards, and Neeltje, who had taken her remark seriously, took her arm, and began to warn her of the dangers of too much sightseeing all at once. They were close to the theatre unit doors when they were flung wide with a good deal of force and Professor ter Bavinck came through them. He was in theatre kit again, his mask dangling under his unshaven chin. He looked tired, cross and even with these drawbacks, very handsome.

Lavinia, watching him coming towards them, was aware of a peculiar sensation, rather as though she had been filled with bubbles and wasn't on firm ground any more, and at the same time she knew exactly what she was going to do. She gently disengaged her arm from Neeltje and walked briskly forward to meet the professor. She wasted no time over good mornings or hullos; she planted her small person before his large one so that he was forced to stop, staring at her with tired eyes. She said, not caring if Neeltje heard or not: 'I was very silly last night. Of course I'll marry you.'

She didn't wait for his reply but slid through the theatre doors with a bewildered Neeltje hard on her heels. 'Whatever did you say?' asked her friend. 'I didn't hear.'

'I said I would,' Lavinia told her, hardly aware of what she was saying, her mind completely taken up with the sudden wonder of finding herself in love. She would have liked to have gone somewhere quiet to think about it, instead she found herself laying up for the first case. It wasn't until she was having her coffee, the first case dealt with, the second laid up for and Sister scrubbing, that she had a few minutes in which to think. The delightful, excited elation was still there, although it was marred just a little by the realization that the professor neither expected nor wished her to love him—it really was enough to put any girl off, she thought with a touch of peevishness, but now that she had discovered that she loved him, to marry him would be perfectly all right, or so it seemed to her.

Her feverish thoughts were interrupted by the two nurses having coffee with her. 'There was a patient in the night,' one of them told her, 'a girl with stab wounds, and a laparotomy must be done, you understand. The surgeon is not happy when he looks inside—there is a question of CA—so he calls for Professor ter Bavinck at three o'clock in the morning and they are here for a long time and he finds that it is CA. Is it not sad?'

'Very,' agreed Lavinia. So that was why he had looked so tired... The other nurse spoke. 'And it is not nice for the Prof, for he goes to Brussels this morning—I heard Zuster Smid say so.'

'Oh,' said Lavinia; disappointment was like a physical pain. She added nonchalantly: 'How long for?'

The nurse shrugged. 'Two-three days, perhaps longer, I do not know. There is a seminar... You wish more coffee?'

'No, thanks.' Lavinia felt exactly like a pricked balloon, and it was entirely her own fault for being so stupidly impetuous. As though the professor had been in a hurry to know her answer; he had thought of it as a sensible arrangement between friends with no need to get excited about it. She shuddered with shame at her childish behaviour; quite likely he had been appalled at it. She went back to theatre with the other two girls, and presently, at Zuster Smid's command, scrubbed to take a minor case. It kept her well occupied until dinner time, and because there was a heavy afternoon list, she stayed behind with Neeltje to get the theatre ready. They had just finished when the professor walked in. He was freshly shaven now, his face wore the look of a man who had had a sound night's sleep, he wore a black and white dogtooth checked suit, cut to perfection, and he looked superbly elegant.

He said something softly to Neeltje as he crossed the floor and she smiled widely as she went into the anaesthetic room—which left Lavinia alone behind her draped trolley, thankful that she was masked and gowned and capped so that almost nothing of her showed. He came to a halt a few yards from her so that there was no chance of him sullying the spotlessness around her.

'That was just what I needed,' he declared, and when she looked bewildered: 'This morning. I stayed up half the night wondering if I had been too precipitate—hurrying you along relentlessly, not giving you time to think. I was no nearer a conclusion when I was called in for that poor girl.'

'Oh,' said Lavinia, 'and I've been worrying all the morning, thinking that you might have found me very silly.' And when he smiled and shook his head: 'I thought you were going to Brussels—one of the nurses told me.'

'I'm on my way, I shall be gone two days. When I come back we'll tell Sibby and the rest of them. When are your days off?'

She told him and he nodded. 'Good. I'll take you to see my mother and father.'

This was something she hadn't known about, and the look she gave him was so apprehensive that he burst out laughing. 'Regretting your decision, Lavinia?'

'No, of course not, it's just that I don't know anything about you...'

'We'll have plenty of time to talk, my dear. I must go. *Tot ziens!*'

She was left staring at the gently swinging door. He had been very businesslike; she doubted if many girls had their marriage plans laid before them with such cool efficiency. Come to think of it, he hadn't shown any gratifying signs of satisfaction concerning his—their future. But then why should he? It was, after all, a sensible arrangement between friends.

She was going off duty on the evening before her days off when the hall porter on duty called to her as she crossed the hall. His English was as sparse as her Dutch, but she was able to make out that she was to be at the hospital entrance by nine o'clock the next morning. She thanked him with the impeccable accent Juffrouw de Waal insisted upon, and sped to her room. There was a lot to do; her hair would have to be washed, and since she had nothing else suitable, it would have to be the pink again and that would need pressing. She set about these tasks, daydreaming a little, wondering if Radmer would be glad to see her.

The fine weather held, the morning sun was shining gloriously as she dressed, ate a hurried breakfast and went down to the hospital entrance. The professor was waiting, in slacks and a thin sweater this time. His greeting was cheerful enough although quite lacking in any sentiment.

'Hullo,' he said. 'We'll go back to the house, shall we—we have to talk, you and I.' He got into the car beside her and turned to smile at her. 'We can do that better sitting comfortably and undisturbed. Sibby will be home for lunch. I thought, if you agree, that we might tell her today; she should be the first to know—she and your sister.'

He was a man for getting to the point without any small talk to lead up to it, she perceived. 'Yes, of course I agree,' she told him with composure, 'but I don't think I'd better tell Peta—she might get so excited that she would tell Aunt Gwyneth, and that wouldn't do at all.'

'Well, we'll have to think about that. I should

like you to meet my mother and father today, and as soon as I can get away I'll take you up to Friesland.'

'Friesland? But that's in the north, isn't it? Have you family there?'

'No—a house, left to me by my grandfather. I should like you to see it. I have a sister, by the way, married and living in Bergen-op-Zoom.'

They had reached the house and went inside. The gentle gloom of the hall was cool after the bright sunshine outside; its beauty struck her afresh as they crossed it and entered the sitting-room. Here the doors were open on to the small garden and the room was alight with sunshine and they went to sit by one of the open windows as Mevrouw Pette followed them in with the coffee tray. It wasn't until she had gone and Lavinia had poured the coffee that the professor spoke, and very much to the point.

'It takes a week or two to arrange a marriage in Holland,' he explained, 'so I think we might get started with the formalities today, then we can marry at the first opportunity—there is no point in waiting, is there?' He glanced briefly at her. 'The sooner the better, then we can go over to England and fetch Peta together; that might make things easier for you both.'

She tried to keep her voice as casual as his, just

as though getting married was an everyday occurrence in her life. 'That's awfully kind of you—I'm sure it would. Do—do I have to do anything about our wedding?'

'Not today—you will need your passport later. Church, I take it?'

'Yes, please.'

'We shall have to be married by civil law first, otherwise we shan't be legally man and wife. Shall we keep it as quiet as possible?'

It cost her an effort to agree to this cheerfully. Was he ashamed of her, or did he suppose they would be the subject of gossip? Perhaps she wasn't good enough for his friends—in that case why was he marrying her? There must surely be girls more suitable amongst his acquaintances.

His voice jolted her gently back to her surroundings. 'None of the reasons you are so feverishly examining are the right ones. When I married Helga we had an enormous wedding, hundreds of guests, a reception, wedding bells, presents by the score, but it was only a wedding, not a marriage. Do you understand? This time it will be just us two, marrying each other for sound and sensible reasons, and no phoney promises of love.' His voice was bitter.

He must have been very unhappy for him to sound like that after all those years. She managed a tranquil: 'I understand perfectly. That's what I should like too, and if you don't want to talk about your—your first wife, you don't have to. I daresay if we were marrying for all the usual reasons, I might feel differently about that, but as you say, this is a sensible arrangement between friends. I shall do my very best to help Sibby in every way, you can depend on that, and I'll learn to run your home as you wish it to be run. I'm not much good at parties, but I expect I'll learn. You're quite sure it's what you want? Peta will be an extra mouth to feed, you know, and I should very much like her to have another year at least of schooling—would you mind paying for that?'

He looked amused. 'Not in the least. I should tell you that I'm a wealthy man—money doesn't have to come into it.' He gave her a thoughtful look. 'And you, my dear—you are content? Perhaps it is an odd state of affairs for a girl—to marry and yet not be a wife; I'm being selfish.'

She answered him steadily. 'No, not really, for I am getting a great deal out of it, too. I—I have no prospects; no one has ever asked me to marry him, and if I didn't marry you, I should be hard put to it to get Peta educated. I'm not much of a catch,' she added frankly. 'I hope Sibendina will like the idea.'

He said on a laugh: 'She was the first one to

suggest it, if you remember.' He got up, and the dogs, lying at his feet, got up too. 'Shall we go to the Town Hall and get the preliminaries over?' he asked.

She didn't understand all of what was said when they got there, but it really didn't matter. She stood watching the professor talking to the rather pompous man who asked so many questions, and wished with all her heart that he could love her, even just a little, even though she felt sure that she had enough love for both of them. Of one thing she was sure already; he thought of her as a friend, to be trusted and talked to and confided in, that at least was something. And if he had decided to marry her for Sibby's sake, it was surely better that he should marry her, who loved him so much, rather than some other girl who didn't.

He turned to speak to her and she smiled at him. He had said that she would never be tempted to reach for the moon, but wasn't that exactly what she had done?

CHAPTER FIVE

THEY GOT BACK to the house with just enough time to have a drink before lunch and the return of Sibendina from school, and Lavinia, although outwardly calm, was glad of the sherry to stop the quaking going on inside her. Her companion, she noticed, was sitting back in his chair looking the picture of ease while he drank his gin, just as though the prospect of getting married in a couple of weeks' time had no worries for him at all. She envied him his cool while she kept up a rather feverish chat about nothing in particular, until he interrupted her with a gentle: 'Don't worry, Lavinia—Sibby will be delighted.'

She did her best to believe him while she wished secretly that he might have felt a little more sympathy for her nerves. After all, not every girl found herself in the kind of situation she was in at the moment. And he could have shown some warmth in his feelings towards her...she corrected the thought hastily, for it had made him seem heartless and cold, and he was neither, only most dreadfully businesslike and matter-of-fact about the whole thing. But then she had herself to blame for that.

Perhaps she appeared as businesslike to him as he did to her, even though she loved him, but of course he didn't know that, and never would. She moved restlessly and caught his eye and managed a smile as the door opened and Sibendina came in.

There had been no need to be nervous after all; Sibby paused in the doorway, looking from one to the other of them, then swooped on her father while a flow of excited words poured from her lips. She had turned and engulfed Lavinia, still chattering madly, before the professor said on a shout of laughter: 'And here is poor Lavinia worrying herself sick in case you don't approve!'

His daughter gave Lavinia a quick kiss and a bearlike hug. 'That is absurd—I am so pleased I do not know what I must say.'

'But how did you know?' asked Lavinia.

'But I see your face, of course—and Papa, sitting there looking just as he looks when his work has gone well and he does not need to worry any more.' She sat down on the sofa between their chairs. 'When will you marry? Shall I be a bridesmaid? And Peta, of course—What shall we wear?'

Her father answered her. 'We shall marry just as soon as it can be arranged—it will be very quiet, *liefje*, I think Lavinia doesn't want bridesmaids.' He smiled at Lavinia, who smiled back. Of course she wanted bridesmaids and white silk and a veil and flowers—all girls did, but since he had made it clear that he didn't, she would have to forget all that. She said now: 'I really would like a small wedding, but it would be lovely if you and Peta could have pretty dresses.'

Sibby became enrapt. 'Blue,' she murmured, 'long, you understand, with little sleeves and large floppy hats for us both. Peta and I will go shopping together.' She beamed at Lavinia. 'It is very good to have a stepmother; Papa is a dear, but he is a man—now I shall be able to talk about all the things girls talk about.' She sighed blissfully. 'We shall be most happy. When do we go to fetch Peta?'

'That will have to wait until a day or so before the wedding,' interpolated the professor, 'and Lavinia and I will go—you won't mind that, will you, Sibby? You can make sure that everything is ready for our return.'

His daughter eyed him rebelliously and then giggled. 'Of course, I am stupid—people who are to be married do not like to have companions, do they, so I will not mind at all. I will buy flowers and make the house beautiful and order splendid meals.' She was struck with a sudden idea. 'I will also invite guests—a great many.'

'Oh, no, you don't,' said her father firmly. 'Your

grandmother will do that; I daresay there will be a big party at her house.'

'She does not know about you and Lavinia, Papa?'

'Not yet. We're going to see her and Grandfather when we've had lunch.' He heaved himself out of his chair. 'Shall we go and have it now?'

He took an arm of each of them and they all went into the dining-room where they had a hilarious meal, largely due to Sibendina's high spirits.

The drive to Noordwijk was short, a bare twenty-five miles, a distance which the Bentley swallowed in well-bred, silent speed. Lavinia was surprised to see that the town appeared to be little more than a row of rather grand hotels facing the sea, but presently they turned away a little and drove through the small town and took a tree-lined road leading away from its centre. Large villas lined it at intervals and she supposed that Radmer's parents lived in one of them, but he didn't stop, leaving them behind to cross the heath, slowing down to drive over a sandy lane which presently led through open gates into the well laid out grounds of a low solidly built house facing the sea. He stopped before its open front door and giving Lavinia no time to get nervous, whisked her out of the car and into the house, and still holding her arm, walked her across the wide hall and through a pair of doors at the back. The room they entered ran across the width of the house so that it had a great many windows overlooking a delightful garden. There were doors too, flung open on to a verandah, its striped awning casting a pleasant shade on to the chairs scattered along its length. The professor wasted no time on the room, but strode rapidly across it and through to the verandah, to stop by the two people sitting there.

Lavinia had no difficulty in recognizing them; the professor's father might be white-haired and a little gaunt, but in his younger days he must have had his son's good looks—even now he was quite something. And his mother, although she was sitting, was a big, tall woman, considerably younger than her husband, with quite ordinary features redeemed by a pair of sparkling blue eyes, as heavy-lidded as her son's. She looked up now and smiled with pleased surprise, and her 'Radmer!' was full of delight as she said something in Dutch in a soft, girlish voice. He bent to kiss her, still with a hand tucked firmly in Lavinia's arm, shook his father by the hand and spoke in English.

'I want you to meet Lavinia—Lavinia Hawkins. She came from England to work at St Jorus a short while ago.' He paused and they greeted her kindly, speaking English as effortlessly as their own tongue, then embarked on small talk with a total

lack of curiosity as to who she was and why she
was there. Perhaps presently they would ask questions, but now they sat her down between them,
plied her with iced lemonade and discussed the
summer weather, the garden, and the delights of
living close to the sea. Lavinia had pretty manners.
She took her share of the conversation while she
wondered why Radmer hadn't dropped at least a
hint about their approaching marriage. Surely he
wasn't going to keep his parents in the dark about
it? She couldn't believe it of him, and her sigh of
relief when he at last spoke was loud enough for
him to hear and glance at her with a smile of un-
derstanding.

There had been a pause in the conversation and
old Mijnheer ter Bavinck had suggested that his
son might like to accompany him to his study, so
that they might discuss some interesting article or
other. Radmer got to his feet, pulled Lavinia gently
to hers too and turned to face his parents.

'My dears,' he said quietly, 'I think you will
have guessed that Lavinia is someone special; we
hope to be married within a very short time.'

There was no doubt of their pleasure. There
were congratulations and kisses and handshakes,
and Mevrouw ter Bavinck picked up a handbell in
order to summon a rather staid, middle-aged
woman and give her some low-voiced instructions,

at the same time telling her the news. She turned to Lavinia as the woman went to wring Radmer's hand and then did the same for Lavinia. 'This is Berthe,' she explained. 'She has been with us since Radmer was a very small boy, so of course she must hear the news too. Joop, her husband, who also works for us, is going to bring up a bottle of champagne.'

She beamed down at Lavinia and touched her lightly on the arm. 'We will allow the men to go away and discuss their dull business; you and I will talk—for now that you are to be our daughter, I may ask you questions, may I not?'

'Of course, Mevrouw ter Bavinck.' Lavinia warmed to the older woman's charm. 'I hope I haven't been too much of a surprise. It—it happened rather suddenly, I'm still surprised myself.'

They were sitting opposite each other now, and her hostess gave her a thoughtful look. 'It has been my dearest wish that Radmer should marry again. Has he told you about Helga—his first wife?'

'Not a great deal, and I told him that if he didn't want to talk to me about her, I wouldn't mind. Should I know?'

Mevrouw ter Bavinck looked doubtful. 'I think you should, but that is something which you will decide between you. But there is one thing, my dear, and you must forgive an old woman's impertinence in asking such a question, but it is important to me—after Helga. Do you love Radmer?'

Lavinia met the blue gaze squarely. 'With all my heart.'

Her companion sighed contentedly. 'That is good—and you will need all that love, Lavinia; he has been a solitary man for more than ten years, he is not young, and he has lived for his work— Now he will live for you, of course, but perhaps he may not realize that just yet.'

Her future mother-in-law was a wise woman who perhaps saw more than she was expected to see. Lavinia said gently: 'He loves Sibendina.'

'Very much, and she, thank God, is wholly his daughter.' The blue eyes twinkled. 'You will be a very young mother for her, but just what she needs. And now tell me, my dear, have you family of your own?'

Lavinia told her about Peta and her parents and Aunt Gwyneth; she found it easy to do this because her listener had the gift of listening as well as putting others at their ease; by the time the two men, followed by the champagne, returned, the two ladies were firm friends, and as Radmer sat himself down close to Lavinia, his mother remarked: 'You are both right for each other, Radmer—I believe you will be very happy. Is the wedding to be a quiet one?'

They drank their champagne and talked in a pleasant desultory way about the marriage, and presently they went into the sitting-room and had tea and small crisp biscuits, and this time Lavinia found herself sitting with Radmer's father, answering his questions, warmed by his kindness.

They got up to go shortly after, with a promise to come again very soon, so that the details of the wedding might be finalized, and when they were once more in the Bentley, driving slowly this time, the professor asked:

'Well, Lavinia, do you think you will like my parents?'

She felt a little tired after the day's excitement, but content too. The answer she gave him must have satisfied him, for he said: 'Good girl, they like you too—I knew they would.'

Which, she supposed with faint bitterness, was, from him, a compliment.

They went out to dine later, but not before he had taken her to a small room at the back of the hall she hadn't previously been into, and opened a drawer in a charming medallion cabinet set against one of its silk-hung walls. The box he took from it was small and leather-covered and when he opened it she saw that it held a ring; a diamond cluster in a cup setting, the gold heavily engraved. He put the box down and came towards her with the ring in the palm of his hand and they looked at it together for a few moments. 'It has been in my mother's family for years,' he said at length. 'I should like you to have it. It hasn't been worn for a long time, for Helga refused to wear it, she considered it old-fashioned.'

Lavinia held up a small, capable hand. It was a pity that Helga had to be dragged into it, but she supposed she was being given the ring for appearances' sake, and anyway, he would have no idea that she was already fiercely jealous of his first wife—indeed, if he found that out, he might cry off, appalled at the very idea of her feeling anything at all but a comfortable, uncomplicated friendship for him. She thanked him nicely, admired the ring, remarked upon its excellent fit, and when he bent and kissed her cheek, received the salute with what she hoped was a warm but not too warm manner. Apparently it was satisfactory, for Radmer took her arm as they went back into the hall, and remarked with some satisfaction that he had no doubt that they would be excellent friends. He even halted half-way to the staircase to say: 'You see, if no emotions are involved, my dear, the success of our marriage is assured; we shall have no bouts of jealousy or imagined feelings of neglect, and no wish to interfere with each other's lives.' He smiled down at her and kissed her for a second time, still on her cheek. 'You do understand that I am deeply engrossed in my work?' he wanted to know.

She said that yes, she quite understood that, and wondered for the first time, deep in her heart, if she would be able to endure living with him in such a manner, but it was a little late to think of that now, and at least she would make him happier than a girl who didn't love him. The thought consoled her as she went upstairs to tidy herself for their evening out.

Time telescoped itself after that evening; some days she didn't see Radmer at all, some days she spent an hour or so at his house or snatched a brief meal with him somewhere, and several times they drove to see his parents.

She had found that, without bothering her with details, he had smoothed the way for her to leave the hospital. All the tiresome formalities had been taken care of, and when she received her salary he had told her to spend it on herself as he had arranged for her to have an allowance which would be paid into the bank on their wedding day. And he had been of the greatest help in writing to Peta, who, they had decided, wasn't to be told anything until they actually arrived at Aunt Gwyneth's house. Lavinia had composed a careful letter, full of optimism about the future, and had told Peta that if she didn't write again for a little while it was because she was going to be busy. She read it out to Radmer on one of their rare evenings together and looked at him anxiously when she had done so. 'Does it sound all right?' she wanted to know. 'And are you sure we're doing the right thing?'

He had reassured her with a patience which soothed her edginess, and when Sibendina had joined them later, he had taken care to keep the conversation light and cheerful, so that she had gone back to hospital and slept like a contented child.

She was still working, of course. Radmer had asked her if she wished to leave St Jorus and she had no doubt that if she had said yes, he would have arranged it for her without fuss or bother, just as he had arranged everything else, but she had chosen to stay on until a few days before they were to marry, going on duty each day, an object of excited attention from her new friends in the hospital.

It was a few days before she was due to leave that Radmer had driven her up to Friesland. They had left very early in the morning, before breakfast, and done the eighty odd miles in under two hours, to eat that meal upon their arrival. Lavinia had been a little overawed at the sight of the large square house set in its small estate to the north of

Leeuwwarden. The grounds around it were beautifully laid out with banks of flowers screened by a variety of shrubs and trees, and a freshly raked gravel drive leading from the great iron gateway at the roadside.

The housekeeper had come to welcome them—Juffrouw Hengsma, a tall, homely woman who said little but smiled her pleasure at seeing them before serving the breakfast they didn't hurry over. Lavinia sat listening to Radmer's history of the house and then spent the remainder of the morning going over it with him, lingering over its treasures of silver and glass and porcelain, and admiring the splendid hangings at the windows and the well-polished furniture. But it was a very comfortable house too, for all its age and size. There were easy chairs and sofas and pretty table lamps scattered around the rooms, thick carpets on the floors, and even though each apartment had an enormous chandelier hanging from the centre of its high ceiling, there was an abundance of wall lighting so that even on the gloomiest day, the rooms would glow with soft light.

'You like it?' asked Radmer, and smiled warmly at her when she declared that she had never seen anything as beautiful. 'Except for your house in Amsterdam,' she added. 'I love it.'

'So do I. We come up here quite often, though. Come and see the garden.'

It was a happy day for her, at any rate, and she thought Radmer had been happy too; she had wanted to be reassured about that quite badly and it had been a good test, spending the whole day together like that, with nothing much to do and only each other to depend upon for company. Looking back, she was as sure as she could be that he had enjoyed being with her—they had found a great deal to talk about and they had discovered similar tastes and ideas. She had gone to bed that night full of hope.

She left the hospital two days later, early in the morning, so that they could catch a Hovercraft at Calais and be at Cuckfield by the afternoon, and although it wasn't yet eight o'clock, she had a tremendous send-off when Radmer came to collect her with the Bentley. He had laughed and waved good-naturedly at the small crowd of nurses, then glanced sideways at her. 'That's a new outfit,' he remarked. 'I like it.'

The sun, already shining, seemed to shine a little brighter; it was a good beginning to a day of which Lavinia felt a little uncertain. 'I'm glad,' she said happily. 'I went to Metz and Metz yesterday and bought some clothes...'

'A wedding dress?' he asked lightly.

'Well, yes.' It had been more expensive than she had expected, but the simplicity of the rich cream crêpe had seemed just right, and she had bought a hat too, covered in cream silk roses. She only hoped that it wouldn't seem too bridal for his taste. She looked down at the blue and white coat dress she was wearing, satisfied for once that she was in the forefront of fashion. She had bought blue sandals too and a leather handbag, and now she had very little money left.

It occurred to her at that moment that Radmer had said nothing at all about a honeymoon; perhaps the Dutch didn't have them, possibly he felt it would be a waste of time. Honeymoons were for people in love, although surely two friends could go on holiday together, and if anyone else wanted to call it a honeymoon, they were at liberty to do so.

They were already out of Amsterdam and as though he had read her thoughts, he asked: 'Would you mind very much if we go straight home after the wedding? I'm up to my ears in work and there's a lecture…'

Her pride wouldn't allow him to finish, to seek more excuses. 'Of course I don't mind—I'll have Peta and Sibby and that lovely house to explore and I shall go shopping.'

He nodded and they didn't talk about themselves

or the wedding again. It was much later, when they were leaving Dover behind them, that she asked: 'I expect you know where Cuckfield is? It's not far.'

'I've driven through it, I believe.' He took the Bentley neatly past a great juggernaut and started down the hill towards Folkestone.

'You know England?'

He smiled. 'I was at Cambridge.'

'Oh, were you?' She added with faint bewilderment: 'I don't know anything about you.'

He laughed. 'It will all come out in good time. Shall we stop for an early lunch? I'm going along the coast road, we could have a meal at the Mermaid in Rye.'

It was during that meal that she asked: 'Which church are we being married at? I did ask you, but if you remember you had to go somewhere or other in a hurry before you could tell me.'

He looked rueful. 'What you mean is, I forgot all about it. I'm sorry—I'm not proving very informative, am I? You wanted somewhere quiet, didn't you, so I've arranged it at the English church in the Begijnsteeg—I hope you'll like that.'

Her face showed that she did. 'An English service? How nice, now I can wear my ring on my left hand...'

He laughed again, very softly. 'If it makes you

feel more securely married, why not? I thought we might go straight there after we've had the civil wedding. Mama is giving a small reception for us afterwards at Noordwijk and the two girls are going to stay there for a couple of days. We can be back home again in the early evening.' She could almost hear relief in his voice at the thought of getting it all over and done with as speedily as possible. It surprised her when he leaned across the table and took her hand in his. 'Have you ever thought how appropriately you are named, my dear?'

She shook her head, conscious of his hand, wishing very much to clasp it with her own.

'Lavinia was the second wife of Aeneas.'

'Oh—Greek mythology.' She furrowed her forehead in thought. 'But my name isn't appropriate at all—I've just remembered, wasn't there someone called Thompson who quoted something about the lovely young Lavinia, and I'm not lovely; I remember my father telling me about it and laughing...'

He said very gently: 'Kind laughter, I'm sure, and there are a great many variations on that word, you know—amiable, sweet, angelic...'

If he had loved her—been in love with her, he wouldn't have needed to say that; she winced at the pain his words had given her and smiled back at him. 'I hope you don't suppose me to be an-gelic? I can be as cross as two sticks sometimes.'

'I know. The first time you spoke to me you were just that. It intrigued me even before I turned round to look at you. I knew you would be differ-ent from other girls.'

Her voice was unconsciously wistful. 'I'm just the same inside,' but she smiled widely as she spoke, just to let him see that she wasn't taking their conversation seriously.

They drove on presently and the nearer they got to Cuckfield, the more nervous Lavinia became, twisting her lovely ring round and round her finger, opening and shutting her handbag for no reason at all, and Radmer, who had shown no sign of nerves, smiled a little to himself, ignoring her small fidgets until on the outskirts of the little town he slowed the car and stopped in a layby, and when she looked at him inquiringly, said mildly: 'Look, Lav-inia, I know how you feel, but will you stop wor-rying and leave it all to me?'

She nodded wordlessly. He would, without doubt, sail through the awkward situation without any outward sign of ill-humour, whatever Aunt Gwyneth said to him. Indeed, he looked capable of moving a mountain if he had a mind to; he also looked very handsome and impeccably turned out. He was wearing the dog-tooth check again with a silk shirt and a tie of sombre magnificence. She had no doubt that he would get his own way without difficulty, whatever obstacle was put in his path.

And she was right. Aunt Gwyneth was at home, having just finished lunch, and was taken completely by surprise. They listened to her blustering efforts to prevent Peta going with them until Radmer settled the matter with a suave confidence which left her shaken.

'There can be no objection,' he pointed out firmly. 'You are not Peta's guardian, and now that Lavinia and I are to be married and can offer her a good home, I can see no reason for your objection. You have yourself just said that she has cost you a great deal and forced you to make sacrifices. I imagine that you have no plans for Peta's future?'

Aunt Gwyneth eyed him angrily. Her plans, such as they were, would have been torn to shreds by this quiet, dreadfully self-possessed man. She made an exasperated sound and turned her spite on Lavinia, sitting as quiet as a mouse, feeling sick. 'Well, it didn't take you long to find yourself a husband, did it?' she demanded. 'And now I suppose all my kindness and money will have been wasted on the pair of you.'

'I can't remember you spending any money on me, Aunt,' Lavinia said with spirit, 'and Peta's school fees can't have been all that much—Father said you had more money than you knew what to do with.' She added bitterly: 'And I can't remember you being kind.'

'Then we can take the matter as settled,' the professor interrupted quietly. 'You will be glad to be rid of your burden, Mrs Turner, and if you have incurred expense beyond your means, I shall be glad to reimburse you.'

Aunt Gwyneth sniffed angrily. 'Indeed I shall...' she began, and got no further as the door opened and Peta came into the room. 'There's a gorgeous Bentley outside—Lavinia!' She flung herself into her sister's arms. 'Lavinia, you said you'd come and I knew you would—oh, dear, I'm going to howl. You will take me with you...?'

Lavinia gave her sister a hug and turned her round. 'Yes, darling—we have just been talking to Aunt Gwyneth—and this is Radmer, we're going to be married in two days' time and you're coming to live with us.'

Peta crossed the room and gazed into his imperturbable face. 'Of course, the Bentley. However did Lavinia find you? You're super!'

He took her hand and said gravely: 'Hullo, Peta, and thank you. Lavinia didn't find me, I found her.'

She was still staring at him. 'What shall I call you?'

'Won't Radmer do? I've a daughter, you know, she's fourteen, and she calls your sister Lavinia, so that makes it right, doesn't it?'

She nodded and smiled then. 'I like you,' she told him shyly. 'Can we go now?'

He looked over her head and smiled faintly, but it was to Mrs Turner, sitting ignored, to whom he spoke. 'Perhaps if Lavinia might pack Peta's things? We don't wish to take up too much of your time.' He spoke with the utmost politeness, quite sure that he would have his way. Apparently Aunt Gwyneth thought so too, for she said angrily: 'Lavinia can do what she likes; she's always an ungrateful, sullen girl. I'm surprised you're going to marry her—she's plain enough, and I can't think what you can see in her.'

The politeness was still there, tinged with arrogance now. 'Probably not, Mrs Turner, but I must remind you that you are speaking of my future wife.' He looked at Lavinia and smiled, warmly this time. 'Perhaps if Peta goes with you?' he suggested. 'She need only bring the things she treasures—we'll buy anything she needs.'

It took ten minutes. Peta had few possessions and a small wardrobe, the two girls packed a case, talking in excited snatches, and went back to the drawing-room where they found their aunt angrily firing questions at Radmer, who was answering them with a patience and ease of manner which Lavinia couldn't help but admire. He got up as they entered the room, took the case from her, stood silently while they wished their aunt good-bye and then offered his own farewells, but all Aunt Gwyneth said was: 'Don't come running back to me, either of you—you would have had a secure home here, Lavinia, as my companion, but if you're fool enough to marry a foreigner...'

Lavinia rounded on her. 'Aunt Gwyneth, don't you dare speak of Radmer in that fashion! He's a good, kind man and we shall be very happy.'

She went through the door Radmer was holding open for her, her cheeks fiery, her head high, and allowed him to settle her in the car without looking at him. Only when he got in beside her did she whisper: 'Oh, I'm so ashamed—she had no right...'

His hand covered hers for a brief moment. 'Thank you, dear girl,' then he took it away and turned to look at Peta, bouncing with impatience on the back seat. 'We're going to spend the night in London. I thought we might go to a theatre this evening, and if we don't stop on the way for tea I think there might just be time for you girls to do some shopping.'

It was Peta who answered him. 'I say, you are super. What sort of shopping?'

'Well, a dress for this evening, perhaps. How about Harrods?'

Peta made a small ecstatic sound and Lavinia murmured: 'But we shan't have time. I thought we were going to spend the night at Dover—I haven't anything with me, only night things.'

'Then you must have a new dress too.'

'Oh, Lavinia, yes!' Peta had leaned forward to poke her pretty face between them. 'Oh, isn't this marvellous? I simply can't believe it! And now tell me about the wedding and where you live and your daughter's name, and am I to go to school…?'

He laughed. 'Lavinia, I leave it to you. See how much you can get into the next half hour.'

Almost everything; enough to satisfy Peta and make her sigh happily. By the time they reached Knightsbridge and Harrods, she was starry-eyed.

It was surprising how much shopping could be done in a short space of time when one didn't need to look too closely at the price tags, and there was someone waiting with a cheque book to pay. They had begun by looking at the less expensive dresses; it was Radmer who had got up from the chair he had taken in the middle of the salon, caught Lavinia by the hand, and pointed out several models which had taken his fancy. She had tried them on, not daring to ask their price, and when she had been unable to decide which of them she preferred—the apricot silk jersey or the grass green patterned crêpe, he had told her to have them both. She went and stood close to him, so that no one should hear, and murmured: 'Radmer, they're frightfully expensive...'

His blue eyes twinkled kindly. 'But you look nice in them,' he pointed out, 'so please do as I ask,' and when she thanked him shyly he only smiled again and then said briskly: 'Now where is Peta—for heaven's sake don't let her buy black with frills.'

But Peta, though young, had as good a taste as Lavinia. She had picked out a cotton voile dress in a soft blue, a Laura Ashley model, and came hurrying to display it. 'Only I don't know how much it is,' she said in a loud whisper, 'and I don't like to ask.'

Radmer settled himself in his chair. 'Try it on,' he suggested. 'I'm sure it's well within my pocket.'

She looked sweet in it, and when he suggested that they might as well buy shoes while they were there, Lavinia gave in, but only because Peta would have been disappointed if she had refused. They were going through the shop when he whispered in her ear: 'It's quite proper, you know, a man may give his future wife anything he chooses.

You mustn't forget that we are to be married in two days' time.'

As though she could forget! She smiled and thanked him and turned to admire the sandals Peta had set her heart on.

She had no idea where they were to stay the night. It was Peta who recognized the hotel. 'Claridges!' she breathed. 'I say, how absolutely super. Are you a millionaire, Radmer?'

He chuckled. 'Not quite. Out you get.'

They had a belated tea before they went to their rooms. Lavinia gasped when she saw the luxury of her room, with its bathroom, and Peta's room on the other side. She changed, constantly interrupted by visits from her excited sister, who was full of questions, when Radmer came across from his room on the other side of the corridor to take them down to dinner—a merry meal, but how could it be otherwise, with Peta chattering so happily? They were enjoying their sorbets when she leaned across the table to say: 'Radmer, what a lucky man you are—you've got everything you want, and now you've got Lavinia too, you must be wildly happy.'

Lavinia found herself listening anxiously for his reply. 'Isn't it apparent?' he asked lightly. Which was a most unsatisfactory answer.

They went to a musical show, an unsophisticated

entertainment which Lavinia suspected must have bored Radmer for most of the time, but it was entirely suitable for Peta's youthful ears and eyes, and she thanked him warmly when they got back to the hotel, and when she had gone to bed, Lavinia thanked him once more for taking Peta under his wing. 'It's like a dream,' she told him, 'and everything has happened so quickly, it doesn't seem quite real.'

He touched her cheek with a gentle finger. 'It's real, my dear.' He spoke so softly that she exclaimed: 'Oh, Radmer, are you sorry that…? Do you want to change your mind…? It would be all right, truly it would. I can't think why you chose me in the first place.'

He took her hands in his, there in the empty corridor outside her room. 'Don't be a goose! I'm not sorry and I don't want to change my mind, although, like you, I'm not quite sure why I chose you.'

He bent to kiss her and wished her good night and she slipped into her room, glad that Peta was already asleep. It was silly to cry about nothing, and that was what she was doing. She told herself that over and over again before she at last fell asleep.

CHAPTER SIX

LAVINIA WAS curled up in a corner of one of the great sofas in the drawing-room of the Amsterdam house, leafing through a pile of magazines, and opposite her, sitting in his great wing chair, was Radmer, reading his post. They had been married that morning, and as she stole a quick glance at him, the wry thought that anyone coming into the room might have mistaken them for an old married couple crossed her mind. She dismissed it at once as being unworthy. No one could have been kinder than Radmer during the last two days, and at least he liked her, she thought bleakly. He had considered her every wish and his generosity had been never-ending. She turned a page and bent her head, pretending to read while she reflected on the past forty-eight hours or so. She was bound to admit that everything had gone splendidly. They had arrived back with Peta to find Sibby waiting for them, and the liking between the two girls had been instantaneous and genuine; she had felt almost sick with relief, and Radmer, who had been watching her, had flung an arm around her shoulders and observed easily: 'Exactly as I anticipated;

they're just right for each other—give them six
months and they'll be as close as sisters.'

Lavinia had been grateful for his quick under-
standing, but when she had tried to thank him he
had stopped her with a careless word and gone on
to talk about something quite trivial. And that
night, after the hilarious dinner they had shared
with the girls, he had taken her to spend the night
with an aunt of his—a nice old lady living on the
other side of Amsterdam in a massive house furnished in the heavy style of Biedermeier. She had
been surprised at being whisked off in that fashion;
quite under the impression that she would stay in
Radmer's house. It was only after he had left her
with Mevrouw Fokkema that that lady had remarked in her slow, careful English: 'It is correct
that you stay here until your marriage, my dear—
we are an old-fashioned family, but we all know,
and dear Radmer too, what is due to a ter Bavinck
bride.'

Lavinia, somewhat taken aback, had smiled and
agreed, and wished that her betrothed had taken
leave of her with a little more warmth; his casual:
'See you tomorrow, Lavinia,' had sounded positively brotherly.

But the next day had been all right. He had
fetched her after breakfast and although he had
been at the hospital most of the day, she and the

two girls had gone shopping together and come home laden with parcels and talking excitedly about the wedding; at least Peta and Sibby had; Lavinia had been wholly occupied in overcoming a severe attack of cold feet... She thought that she had concealed her apprehension rather well, but that evening, when the girls had gone to Sibby's room to try on their new dresses and she had found herself alone with Radmer, he had asked quietly: 'Wanting to cry off, Lavinia?'

She had put down the letters she had been reading, and because she was an honest girl, had given him a straight look and said at once: 'No, not that—I think I'm a little scared of all this...' She waved an arm at the splendid room they were in. 'I'm afraid I shall let you down, Radmer.'

'Never!' He was emphatic about it. 'And it isn't as though I have quantities of friends, you know— I've friends enough, but most of them are sober doctors and their wives, and I don't entertain much.' For a moment he looked bleak. 'Helga entertained a great deal—she liked that kind of life; the house always full of people—and such people!' He blinked and smiled. 'Mind you, we shall have to do our best for Sibby and Peta in a year or two, but I think you like a quiet life, too, don't you?'

She imagined herself as he must think of her— a home body, content to slip into middle-age, running his house with perfection and never getting between him and his work. The hot resentment had been bitter in her mouth even while she knew that she had no right to feel resentful.

Her rather unhappy musings were interrupted by his quiet: 'You haven't turned a page in five minutes, Lavinia,' so that she made haste to throw him a warm smile and a cheerful: 'I was thinking about today; trying to remember your family—it was all so exciting.' She thought she had convinced him, for he smiled a little and commented: 'The kind of wedding I like,' before he picked up the next letter and became absorbed in it.

Lavinia put down her magazine, picked up her letters again, and re-read them before casting them down once more and choosing another magazine. She must remember to turn the pages this time, while she let her thoughts wander. If I were a raving beauty, she pondered sadly, we wouldn't be here; he wouldn't be reading his letters—we'd be out dancing, or going for a trip round the world, or buying me lashings of diamonds and clothes, just because he loved me. She jumped when he spoke with sudden urgency: 'Good lord, I quite forgot!' and went out of the room, to return almost at once with a jeweller's velvet case in his hand. 'A wedding present,' he explained, and opened it to take out a pearl necklace and stoop to clasp it round her neck. She put a surprised hand up to feel its silky smoothness and then looked up at him. His face was very close; she kissed him on a hard cheek and said in a wondering voice: 'Oh, Radmer, for me? Thank you—they're beautiful!' She managed a smile. 'Now I feel like the Queen...and you've given me so much!'

She was thinking of the new cheque book in her handbag and the abundance of flowers in her beautiful bedroom, the accounts he had opened for her at several of the fashionable shops, and last but not least, the gold wedding ring he had put on her finger that morning.

He stood up, said to surprise her: 'You're a very nice girl, Lavinia,' and went to sit down again and pick up the *Haagsche Post*, which left her with nothing to do but sit and think once more.

Their wedding had been a happier and gayer affair than she had anticipated; she hadn't expected quite as many people, but then she hadn't known that Radmer had such a large family or so many old friends. She had dressed at his aunt's house and he had come to fetch her with his offering of flowers—roses and orchids and orange blossom in creamy shades to match her gown—and they had driven together, first to the civil wedding and then to the little church in the peaceful Beguinehof, where they had been married again, this time by the English chaplain. It wasn't until they had stood together in the old church that she had felt really married.

They had driven to Noordwijk after that, to the reception Radmer's mother had arranged for them, and where she had met aunts and uncles and cousins and watched Peta and Sibby flitting amongst the guests, having the time of their lives. At least the two girls were blissfully happy. Sibby had hugged and kissed her and declared that she looked super and would make a marvellous mother, and Peta had kissed her and whispered: 'Oh, Lavinia, I'm so happy! Who could have dreamt that this would happen—aren't you crazy with joy?'

Lavinia assured her that she was, and it was true—she was; life wasn't going to be quite the wonder-world it might have been, but at least she could do her best to be a good wife. She turned a page, mindful of his watchful eye. If this was what he wanted then she would do her best to give it to him; peace and quiet at home and a self-effacing companionship. It sounded dull, but it wouldn't be; they got on well together, she knew that for certain; the drive back from Noordwijk had been relaxed and pleasant, even amusing. Dinner had been fun too, with champagne and Lobster Thermidor and an elaborate dessert in her honour.

She turned another unread page and glanced at

the clock—a magnificent enamel and ormolu example of French art. It was barely ten o'clock, but probably Radmer was longing to go to his study and work on the pile of papers which never seemed to diminish on his desk. Lavinia said good night without fuss, thanked him again for the pearls, and walked to the door.

He reached it before she did, to open it for her, and then, just as she was passing through, caught her by the shoulder. 'I enjoyed my wedding,' he told her soberly, 'and I hope you did too. Anyone else but you would have felt hard done by, coming back on your wedding day to sit like a mouse, pretending to read...' His eyes searched her face. 'I've not been fair to you, Lavinia.'

'Of course you have.' She was glad to hear her voice so matter-of-fact. 'You explained exactly how it would be when you asked me to marry you.' She drew a sharp breath. 'It's what I want too,' she told him steadily.

He bent and kissed her. 'You understand, don't you? You're the only girl I felt I wanted for a wife without getting involved—I've known that since the moment we met. I've built a good life, Lavinia, and a busy one, my work is important to me, you know that, and now we will share that life, but only up to a point, you know that too, don't you?'

'Oh, yes. I don't know much about it, but I can

guess that losing your—your first wife made you so unhappy that you've shut the door on that side of your life—there—the loving part. I'll not open that door, Radmer.' She smiled and asked lightly: 'May I have breakfast with you? I'm used to getting up early—besides, I've an English lesson tomorrow morning with Juffrouw de Waal—she was annoyed because I've missed several just lately.' She nodded brightly at him, crossed the hall and started up the stairs. At the top she turned to lift a hand. The smile she had pinned on her face was still there, and he was too far away to see the tears in her eyes.

She didn't sleep much, but she was up early to bathe her puffy eyelids and rub the colour back into her cheeks, and when she went downstairs she looked just as usual; a little pale perhaps, but that was all. She was wearing the blue and white dress and sandals on her bare feet, and when Radmer saw her as he came in from the garden with the dogs, he wished her a cheerful good morning and said how nice she looked. 'It's going to be a hot day,' he remarked, 'and you look delightfully cool.' They walked together to the small room at the back of the house where they were to have breakfast, his arm flung round her shoulders. 'I've a busy day,' he told her as they sat down. 'Don't expect me back for lunch, but with luck I'll be home about four o'clock, and if you feel like it, we might go out for dinner.'

She poured their coffee carefully. 'That would be delightful—but can you spare the time?'

He looked up from the letters he was examining, his eyes narrowed, but she had been innocent of the sarcasm he had suspected. He said blandly: 'My dear, you had the shabbiest treatment yesterday evening, and we aren't going away for a holiday; the least I can do is to take you out and about—besides, I should like very much to do that. We'll go to the Amstel and dine on the terrace overlooking the canal—you'll enjoy that, and tomorrow evening I've booked a table at the Hooge Vuursche Hotel. It's near Baarn—we might dance as well as dine there.'

Her eyes sparkled. 'It sounds fun. Are they very smart places?'

He took his cup from her. 'Yes, I suppose so. Why not go out after your session with Juffrouw de Waal and buy a couple of pretty dresses? I like you in pink.' He picked up the first of his letters. 'You looked pretty in that cream silk dress, too.'

She said thank you in a contained little voice; a triumph, albeit a small one—he had noticed what she was wearing and liked it. 'I'll go along to the Leidsestraat, there's a boutique—oh, and Kraus en Vogelzang in Kalverstraat...' She saw that he wasn't listening any more, but frowning over a sheaf of typewritten pages. Someone had placed a *Daily Telegraph* by her place. She poured herself some fresh coffee and began on its headlines.

Juffrouw de Waal received her sternly, only relaxing sufficiently to congratulate her on her marriage, observe that the professor was a fine man and deserved a good wife, and point out that now Lavinia was that wife, it behoved her to learn Dutch in the quickest possible time.

'And not only conversation, Mevrouw ter Bavinck,' she pointed out soberly. 'It is necessary that you read, and understand what you read, so that you may take part in talk of a serious nature—politics, for instance, as well as the day-to-day events in our country—the world too. You must also learn about our prices and the keeping of accounts as well as how to order household requirements. I suggest that you read a small portion of a daily newspaper to me, which you will translate and discuss in Dutch, and I hope that you will use every opportunity to speak our language.'

Thus admonished, Lavinia applied herself to her lesson with more enthusiasm than ever before; how pleased Radmer would be when she could discuss the meals with Mevrouw Pette without the aid of dictionary or sign language; lift the receiver off the hook and order the groceries in Dutch; ask him—

in his own language, how his day had gone… Fired
with this praiseworthy desire, she accepted a great
deal of homework from her teacher, promised that
she would see her in two days' time, and made her
way to the Leidsestraat.

It was exciting to examine the elegant clothes in
the shop windows and know that she could buy
any of them if she wished. Finally, she found just
what she was looking for in a boutique; a pink
organza dress with a brief tucked bodice, a deep
square neckline, and elbow sleeves, very full and
caught into satin bands which matched the narrow
band below the bodice. The skirt was wide, the
darker pink roses of the pattern rambling over it.
It was a beautiful dress and very expensive, but
she bought it; she bought a peach-coloured chiffon
which caught her eyes, too—after all, Radmer had
told her to get two dresses and she couldn't wear
the same dress twice running. She shopped for
matching slippers and a white velvet shoulder wrap
which would go nicely with both dresses, and then,
very happy with her purchases, went back to the
house in the square.

She had her lunch, held a long telephone conversation with Peta and Sibby, took the dogs for a
walk and then settled down to wait for Radmer. It
had gone four o'clock when he telephoned; he
would be late—something had turned up, but

would she go ahead and dress? He would be home as soon after six o'clock as he could.

But it was almost two hours until then; she took the delighted dogs for another walk, made herself work at her Dutch lesson, and then at last permitted herself to go to her room and dress. She took a long time about it, trying not to look at the little gilt clock ticking away the minutes so slowly, until finally, complete to the last dab of powder on her ordinary little nose, she went downstairs.

She was half-way down the staircase when Radmer came in, flung his case into the nearest chair and paused to look at her. 'Oh, very nice,' he said, 'very nice indeed. I can see that coming home is going to be a real pleasure now that I have a wife. I like the dress.' He was crossing the hall to meet her as he spoke and took her hands and held her arms wide while he studied her person. She stood quietly, her heart capering around beneath her ribs, making it difficult for her to breathe calmly; all the same she managed a very creditable, 'I'm glad you like it,' and then lost her breath altogether when he suddenly pulled her close and kissed her; not a gentle kiss at all, but fierce and hard.

'I like you too,' he told her, and then: 'I'll be fifteen minutes—pour me a drink while I'm changing, will you? Whisky.'

Lavinia waited for him in the sitting-room, the

whisky ready, and with nothing better to do but wonder why he had kissed her in that fashion, it augured well for their evening—it might even augur well for their future. The memory of the look on his face when he had come home stirred her pulse, and the tiny flame of hope which flickered so faintly, and which she had promised herself she would keep alive at all costs, glowed more strongly, so that when she heard his step in the hall, she turned a smiling face to the door.

He had changed into a dinner jacket and he looked good in it—she saw that with her first glance. The second showed her that whatever feeling had prompted him to kiss her in that fashion had been cast off with his other clothes, without him uttering a word she could see that. So she said hullo with a lightness she didn't feel and added: 'I've poured your drink—it's over there, on the drum table,' and as he went to fetch it: 'Have you had a busy day?'

He went and sat down. 'Yes, there was a heavy list in both theatres—and Mevrouw van Vliet— you remember her?' He began to tell her about the case. 'We did another frozen section, you know— I'm afraid there's nothing much to be done. We had several positives today, too.'

'I'm sorry,' said Lavinia, and meant it. 'It clouds the day, doesn't it?'

He gave her an appreciative glance. 'Yes—but I shouldn't bring my work home with me, I'm afraid it's rather a temptation to talk about it with you—you see I never could…and with Sibby, it's been out of the question, of course.' He smiled a little. 'What have you been doing with yourself? And did the girls telephone?'

She related the peaceful happenings of her own day and passed on the messages Sibby and Peta had sent him, adding: 'They're having a lovely time. Peta says she's never been so happy before in her life, and that's true, you know—when she was a little girl, there was never much money and besides that, Mother wasn't very strong…!'

'And you, Lavinia—were you happy?'

She considered his question. 'For most of the time, I think; at least until Father died.' She got up and straightened a few cushions, wishful to change the conversation. 'I went to the kitchen today,' she told him, 'and Mevrouw Pette and I had a long talk—I had my dictionary, and we got on quite well.'

She succeeded in making him laugh. 'I should have enjoyed the conversation. How is the Dutch coming along?'

'I know a great many words,' she told him hopefully, 'and a few sentences.'

He put down his glass. 'When you know a few

more, we will give a dinner party.' He grinned at her look of horror. 'Don't worry, we'll invite only those who speak English—all the same, you must try and speak Dutch as often as possible.'

She promised him that she would as they walked to the door together and she had the satisfaction of seeing that he was not on his guard with her. The kiss had been a reaction after a bad day, she decided, and he had been afraid that she would take advantage of it, despite what she had told him. She got into the car beside him, determined to be a pleasant, undemanding companion for the rest of the evening.

It was perfect weather and warm. They had a table in the window, where they could watch the barges chugging steadily up and down the canal, and they talked of a great many things while they ate. Radmer, once more his usual friendly, faintly impersonal self, took pains to please her. She had looked at the vast menu in some perplexity until he had suggested that she might like him to choose for her: hors d'oeuvres, Poulet Poule mon Coeur and syllabub, and when he asked her what she would like to drink, she left that to him too and drank the chilled Amontillado and then the white Burgundy with enjoyment, pronouncing the latter to be very pleasant, an innocent remark which caused her husband's mobile mouth to twitch very slightly; the bottle of Corton Charlemagne which he had ordered had been treated with due reverence by the wine waiter, being a wine to be taken seriously, but he only agreed with her and refilled her glass, remarking at the same time that wine was an interesting subject for anyone who cared to learn about it.

Lavinia took a sip and eyed him thoughtfully. 'I expect this is a very good one, isn't it? I don't know one from the other, but I'll have to learn, won't I?' She frowned. 'Would Mevrouw Pette…?'

A smile tugged at the corner of his mouth. 'Well, I daresay she's an authority on cooking sherry and so forth—I'm by no means that myself, but I daresay I could put you on the right track— remind me to do so when we have a quiet evening together.'

They sat over their meal, and as the evening darkened slowly, Lavinia, sitting in the soft glow of the pink-shaded table lamp, her ordinary face brought to life by excitement and the wine, became positively pretty.

'Do you come here often, Radmer?' she asked.

'Occasionally, with friends. I don't—didn't go out a great deal. It must be months since I was here.'

She poured their coffee. 'But the head waiter knew you.'

He chuckled. 'That's his job. Shall we bring the girls here one evening? When is Peta's birthday?'

She told him, smiling with pleasure. 'She'd love it—she hasn't had much fun...' She looked away quickly because of the expression on his face; she didn't quite know what it was, but it might have been pity—it disappeared so quickly that afterwards she told herself that she had imagined it.

They drove back in a companionable silence and when they reached the house she wished him good night at once and went upstairs to bed; probably he had had enough of her company for one evening; she would have to give him time to get used to having her around. He made no effort to detain her and when she had thanked him he had replied that he had enjoyed himself too and looked forward to the following evening.

She knew better than to be chatty at breakfast; she poured his coffee, replied quietly to his query as to whether she had slept well, and sat down to her own meal and the *Daily Telegraph*. Her goodbye was cheerful as he got up to leave her, and she added a: 'And I hope it's a better day for you all,' for good measure as he left the room. She was heartily ashamed of the forlorn tears which dripped down on to her uneaten toast. She wiped them away fiercely, telling herself that she was becoming a regular cry-baby, and then took the dogs for a walk in the park before telephoning Peta and Sibby, who were coming home again on the following day. The pair of them sounded very pleased with life, taking it in turns to talk so that there was very little need for her to say more than a word or two. She put the receiver down at length and went along to find Mevrouw Pette, who had suggested that she might like to go through the linen cupboard with her.

Radmer came home earlier than she had expected him to. She was on her knees in the middle of the sitting-room carpet, the dogs sprawled on either side of her, learning Dutch verbs, when he walked in. The dogs rushed to greet him and she would have got to her feet if he hadn't said at once: 'No, don't move—I'll join you. What on earth are you doing?'

He glanced through the dry-as-dust grammar and shut the book. 'My poor dear,' he observed. 'I had quite forgotten how difficult our language is. Is Juffrouw de Waal a tyrant?'

She giggled. 'Well, yes, a bit. She gave me quite a lecture yesterday, though it was a useful one too…she told me that it was even more necessary that I should master Dutch quickly now that I was married to you. I have to read the papers each day, and translate what I read, so that I can discuss politics with you.'

He shouted with laughter. 'My dear girl, I almost never talk politics, and I should find it boring if you did. I'd rather come home to a wife in a pink dress who listens sympathetically to my grumbles about work and makes sensible comments afterwards.'

She sat back on her heels. 'Did you have a good day?'

He had stretched out beside her, lying full length with his hands behind his head, looking up at her. 'Yes, it was a good day. Have we had tea?'

'No, not yet. I'll ask for it right away. Do you want it here or in your study?'

His eyes were closed, but he opened them to stare at her. When he spoke it was so softly that she almost didn't hear him. 'I like your company, Lavinia—it grows on me—don't ever doubt that; even when I'm irritable or tired or worried—you have the gift of serenity.' He closed his eyes again and added: 'I'm hungry; somehow or other I missed lunch.'

It would have been very satisfying to have asked him what he had meant, instead she whisked down to the kitchen, made herself understood by the co-operative Mevrouw Pette and hurried back to assure Radmer that a sustaining tea was on the way.

It gave her deep satisfaction presently, to watch him make short work of the sandwiches, anchovy toast and wholesome homemade cake Bep brought in a few minutes later, and when he had finished and closed his eyes in a nap, she sat, as still as a mouse, until he opened them again, wide awake at once, to look at the clock and suggest that they should change. 'I've booked a table for half past seven,' he told her, 'it's only half an hour's drive, but I thought it would be nice to sit over our drinks.'

The peach chiffon looked stunning; she did her face with care, brushed her hair until it shone and went downstairs to find him already waiting and any last lingering qualms she might have entertained about the extravagance of purchasing two dresses and expensive ones at that, at the same time, were successfully extinguished by his surprised admiration. 'Very nice,' he commented. 'I liked the pink, but this one is charming.'

'Well, it is a kind of pink,' she told him seriously. 'I didn't really need it, but it looked so pretty and fitted so well...'

He studied her carefully. 'Very well.' He took the wrap from her and put it round her shoulders. 'Remind me to buy you a fur wrap.'

She turned round slowly to face him. 'I wouldn't dream of doing that,' she assured him earnestly.

'Wives don't remind their husbands to buy them things like furs,' and then she giggled when he took his handkerchief out of his pocket to tie a knot in a corner of it. 'Don't be absurd!'

'Ah, but you don't understand, Lavinia. I'm a little out of touch when it comes to remembering what husbands do and don't do—it's been a long time.'

And what, in heaven's name, was a second wife's answer to a remark like that? She decided to ignore it and said instead: 'Shall we go? I'm looking forward to seeing this hotel. I told Sibby that we were going there and she said it was super.'

Sibby had been right; it was a splendid place, a castle once, but now a famous hotel standing in its own grounds, and as the evening was, for once, windless and warm still, they strolled about the terraces and then sat down by one of the fountains for their drinks, and presently, seated at a table by the window so that they had a splendid view of that same fountain, they dined off kipper paté, entrecote sauté Cussy, and crêpes soufflés aux pêches, and as the steak had been cooked with port wine, and the soufflé was flavoured with kirsch and they, in their turn, had been washed down with the excellent claret Radmer had chosen, Lavinia began to enjoy herself, and when he suggested that they might dance, she got up with all the will in the world, determined not to miss anything of her treat. She danced delightfully, and Radmer, after the first few seconds, realized it. He was a good dancer himself—they went on and on, not talking much, sitting down for a drink from time to time and then, by common consent, taking to the floor again. She had been surprised to find that he was as good at the modern dances as the more conservative waltz and foxtrot, and at the end of one particularly energetic session he had said almost apologetically: 'Sibby taught me; I find them rather peculiar, but they're fun sometimes—you're very good yourself.'

'But I prefer waltzing,' said Lavinia, as indeed she did; she could have danced all night and the evening was going so fast—probably once the girls were back home, he wouldn't ask her out again; not just the two of them. Their outings would more than likely be family ones from now on.

They danced a last, dreamy waltz and she went to fetch her wrap. As they got into the car she said: 'That was wonderful, Radmer, thank you for a lovely evening.'

'We'll do it again,' he promised her as he manoeuvred the car on to the road, and Lavinia stifled disappointment because he hadn't said that he had enjoyed it too. She smoothed the soft stuff of her gown, and sat quietly, thinking about the evening, until he broke into her reverie. 'It's a splendid night,' he observed casually. 'We'll go back down the country roads, shall we? There'll be no traffic—we can miss Hilversum completely and work our way round the Loosdrechtsche Plassen, go through Loenen and back on to the motorway below Amstelveen—almost as quick, and far nicer.'

She agreed happily. She wasn't in the least tired, on the contrary, the dancing had left her glowing and wide awake. They talked with idle contentment about nothing in particular as Radmer drove across the golf course, under the motorway and on to the narrow roads which bordered the lakes. They were already two-thirds of the way to Loenen; indeed, Lavinia could make out a few lights, still well ahead of them across the water when, looking idly around her at the quiet, moonlit countryside, she exclaimed suddenly: 'Radmer—that light, over there, on the right…'

'I've seen it, dear girl—a fire, unless I'm mistaken. There's a lane somewhere—here it is.' He swept the big car into a rough, unmade road, a mere cart track. 'This will take us somewhere close, I fancy.'

The fire could be seen more plainly now; a dull glow brightening and fading, almost dimmed by the brilliant moonlight. And it was further away than Lavinia had thought—it must be an isolated farmhouse set well back from the road, in the rough heath bordering the lakes. She fancied she could smell smoke now and hear the faint crackling of fire in the quiet of the night, and presently they had their first real view of the house. A farmhouse, right enough, standing amongst trees and rough grass; the lane they were driving along ended in its yard. Radmer came to a halt well away from the farm buildings, said 'Stay here,' and got out, to disappear quickly through a side door which he had had no compunction in breaking down with a great shoulder. Lavinia could hear him calling and someone answering faintly. She heard other sounds too, now—horses, snorting in fright, and cows bellowing; they would be in the great barn at the back of the house. The fire wasn't visible from where she sat, only a faint flickering at the windows; it might not be too bad at the moment, but by the time Radmer had roused the family, it might be too late to save the animals. She got out of the car and looked about her; she could see no one. She put her handbag and wrap carefully on the car seat, shut the door, and ran towards the barn.

CHAPTER SEVEN

It was easy enough to find the door in its vast side; the moonlight showed Lavinia that—it crept in after her, too, showing her the enormous lofty place, with cow stalls down each side of a wide cobbled path, two horses, giants to her shrinking eyes, stamping and snorting in the partitioned-off stables at the further end. There were a medley of farm carts in another corner, and bales of hay... She wasted no more time in looking, but shaking with fright, went to unbar the great doors opening on to the yard and the fields beyond, and then, uttering loud, encouraging cries, more for her own benefit than those of the beasts, went to untie the horses, relieved to find that despite their fear, they had no intention of kicking her to pieces, merely snorting violently as they backed out of their stable and trotted ponderously out into the yard. She wasn't too keen on cows, either, but she went from one spotless stall to the next, taking down the bars and trusting to their readiness to respond to her pleas that they should bestir themselves. And they did, to her great relief; they hurried, as well as cows will hurry, jostling each other in their common wish to get away from the smell of smoke.

She saw them on their way and then made a cautious round of the vast place to make sure that there was nothing left alive in it. A bull, she thought despairingly—if there's a bull I'll not dare go near it, but there was no bull, only a cow dog, growling at her from his fenced-off pen in a dark corner. Lavinia remembered now that she had heard him barking when she had been seeing to the horses. She went to him at once and started to untie the rope attached to his collar, talking hearteningly the while, so anxious to set him free that she hardly noticed his curled lip. 'Good dog,' she encouraged him as she let him go, still happily unaware of his fierceness, 'run along and look after those cows.' And he rolled a yellow eye at her and went.

The smell of smoke was strong now and wisps of it were oozing through the end wall of the barn. When Lavinia found another small door, obviously leading to the house, and went through it, she was instantly enveloped in a thick smoke which set her coughing and made her eyes smart and water, but there was no going back; she wasn't sure where she was, but Radmer must be somewhere close by and he might be needing help. The thought sent her blundering ahead, out of the worst of the smoke into a comparatively clear space which she took to be a lobby between the kitchen and the front of the house. She could see the fire now and hear it as well; and although the stairs were still intact she saw flames licking the stair head above. There seemed to be no one downstairs. Lavinia started to climb, just as Radmer came carefully down, a child in his arms.

'I told you to stay in the car,' he said calmly, 'but since you're here, will you take this infant? Not injured, just terrified.'

She received the small, shaking form. 'Who else is there?'

'The mother—had a baby yesterday—I'll have to carry them down. The man of the house got up to see what was the matter and was overcome by smoke. I dragged him on to the doorstep.' He grinned at her and went back upstairs.

The farmer was lying outside his front door, recovering slowly, not really aware of her, all the same she told him in a bracing tone as she stepped carefully over him, 'Don't worry, you'll be all right. I'll be back in a minute.'

Lavinia put the child in the back of the car and closed the door on its frightened bawling; she would have liked to have stayed to comfort it, but she had to go back into the house again. Radmer couldn't manage the mother and baby all at once and the fire might get fiercer.

There had been more smoke than flames, but now, looking up the narrow stairs, she could see that the landing was well alight and filled with a thick smoke. She ran through to the kitchen, snatched up a tea towel, wrung it out with furious speed under the sink tap and swathed it round her nose and mouth and then ran upstairs, where she was far more frightened by Radmer's furious look than the fire. 'Get out of here!' he told her furiously. 'You little fool, do you want to be killed?'

'No!' She had to shout because of the tea towel. 'But now I am here, I'll take the baby.'

She snatched the small scrap from the bed and raced downstairs and out to the car, saying 'Excuse me,' politely to the farmer as she stepped over him once more. The baby was whimpering; she laid it on the car's floor, begged the toddler not to cry and went back to the man. He was feeling better, although his colour was bad. '*Mijn vrouw—die kinderen,*' he muttered urgently, and tried to get up. Lavinia didn't know the word for safe, so she smiled, nodded reassuringly and said OK, a useful phrase which she had found of the greatest help since she had arrived in Holland. But he had lapsed into semi-consciousness again and could offer no help as she began to heave him to one side—and only just in time, for a moment later Radmer came through the door with the woman in his arms. Lavinia got to the car ahead of him, flung open the door, whisked up the baby and toddler and hugged them to her while he deposited his burden on the back seat, then handed them over to be tucked in with their mother.

Radmer spoke in a reassuring voice, shut the door again and said briefly:

'See if you can get the man to come round a bit while I get the animals out of the barn.'

'I have.'

He looked at her in astonishment. 'All of them? Cows—horses?'

She nodded. 'And a dog. There's nothing left there, I looked to see.'

He said on a laugh: 'You brave girl—were you frightened?'

'Terrified. The man…?' As he turned away: 'Is there anywhere I can go for help?'

He paused. 'I imagine someone will have seen the fire by now even in this remote area; thank heaven it took its time before it got a hold. If I could get the man on his feet we might save quite a lot of furniture, but we can't put the fire out, I'm afraid.' He gave her a thoughtful look.

'Lavinia, can you drive?'

'Yes. I took lessons and passed my test—ages

ago—I haven't driven more than a couple of times since.'

'Think you can handle the Bentley? I'll reverse her for you—take her back to the road and stop at the nearest house.' He saw the look on her face and went on: 'I know you're scared to do it, my dear, but the woman needs to go to hospital as soon as possible.' He smiled suddenly. 'Do you suppose you could make yourself understood?'

'I'll do my best.'

'Good girl—now let's get the car turned.' He left her for a moment and went to bend over the farmer; when he came back he said: 'I think he'll be all right—I'll get to work on him when you've gone.'

She waited while he turned the Bentley and then got into the driver's seat. He had left the engine running, she only had to drive away... She turned a white face to his as he put his head through the open window.

'Off with you,' he said cheerfully, and kissed her.

She went very slowly at first; the car seemed huge, and although she hadn't forgotten how to drive, she was decidedly slow. But there was nothing to hinder her and the moon was still bright, lighting up the countryside around her. She gained the main road, turned clumsily into it and put her foot down gingerly on the accelerator; there must be something within a mile or so, and at the worst, Loenen was only a short drive away.

The road wound along, close to the water and there were no houses at all, but presently, as she slowed down to take a bend in the road, she saw a massive pair of gates opened on to a drive. The house might be close by; it was worth trying anyway. She edged the Bentley between the posts and sent the car up the tree-shadowed drive, to slither to a halt before a sizeable house, shrouded in darkness. She got out, murmuring reassuringly to the occupants of the back seat, and then turned back to look at the clock on the dashboard. Two o'clock in the morning—whatever would the occupants say? She rang the bell, not waiting to give herself an answer.

The elderly man who came to the door after what seemed a very long time, stood and stared at her in astonishment; as well he might, she conceded. Callers in grubby evening dress didn't usually ring door bells at that hour of night. She wished him good evening, and not wanting to get involved in a conversation she surely wouldn't understand, asked urgently: 'Telephone?' She added helpfully: '*Politie*,' and waved towards the car.

The man gave her a sharp look and spoke at some length until she interrupted him with another urgent 'Telephone?' but he still hesitated, and she was marshalling her Dutch to try again when there were steps behind him and a voice demanded: '*Wat is er aan de hand*?'

'Oh, if only someone could speak English,' cried Lavinia, very much frustrated, and found herself looking over the man's shoulder at a woman's face that smiled at her and asked: 'What is it that you want? You are in trouble?'

'Yes,' said Lavinia, and drew a relieved breath before explaining briefly what had happened. 'And my husband says that the woman must be got to hospital as soon as possible,' she finished. 'Could an ambulance be called?'

The woman smiled again. 'Of course, but first we bring the mother and children in here. Does your husband know where you are?'

Lavinia shook her head. 'No, he told me to go to the first house I saw.'

Her questioner turned to the elderly man and spoke quietly and he went away; Lavinia could hear his voice somewhere inside, presumably telephoning. 'And now the children...' The lady held out a hand, obviously meaning it to be shaken. 'Mevrouw van der Platte.'

It seemed funny to stop for introductions at such a time, but Lavinia shook the hand and murmured: 'Mevrouw ter Bavinck.'

Her hostess's smile broadened. 'The wife of Radmer? We know him slightly.' She nodded her head in a satisfied fashion, pulled her dressing gown more closely round herself and followed Lavinia to the car, and in a moment the elderly man joined them.

Between them they bore the woman and children indoors, into a large hall, comfortably furnished, where the three unfortunates were made comfortable on a large sofa and the elderly man was dispatched to warm some milk.

'My husband is away from home,' explained Mevrouw van der Platte. 'Henk is our houseman, he lives here with his wife, who is the cook, but I think there is no reason to call her. Can I do anything to help you, Mevrouw ter Bavinck?'

Lavinia was bending over her patient, who looked ill and very pale. The toddler was asleep now, and the baby tucked up with his mother.

'I don't think so, thank you. I don't think they have burns, but the smoke was very bad. Will the ambulance and fire engine take long?'

As if in answer to her question she heard the sing-song wail coming towards them along the road, followed by a second. 'Fire engine, police,' said Mevrouw van de Platte unnecessarily, and handed her a glass of warm milk. 'You will want this for your patient. When you have done, there is coffee for you.'

She watched while Lavinia gave the woman the milk. 'Tell me, you saw the fire?'

'We were coming home from Baarn—Radmer thought it would be pleasant to drive through the country roads.'

'And he is there now? At the fire?'

'Yes. If he could get the farmer on to his feet, he thought they might be able to save some of the furniture.'

'The animals?'

'I let them out of the barn—I do hope they won't stray. The dog was with them.'

The companion eyed her with respect. 'You are a sensible girl—your husband must be proud of you.'

Lavinia wiped her patient's mouth and said nothing to that, only: 'I hope he knows where to find me.'

'He will. Henk told the police where you were and they will tell your husband. The ambulance should be here very soon now.'

Radmer got there first, though. Lavinia heard his voice when Mevrouw van der Platte went to answer the door bell. He came in quickly and went at once to her and took her hands. 'You're all right?' he wanted to know, wasting no time in greeting her.

Her heart had given a joyful skip at the sight of him although she answered him calmly enough. 'Yes, thanks—I'm fine, but will you take a look at Mum? I've given her some milk, but she doesn't look too good.'

They were bending over the woman when their hostess came back with a tray of coffee. Radmer straightened himself as she set the tray down. 'She needs treatment—there's an ambulance on the way?'

'Yes—are the babies to go with her?'

'Yes. The father went straight to hospital in one of the police cars—he's all right, but he'll need a check-up. They'll keep him there until they've had a look at this dear soul and the children.'

'Do you want me to go with them?' Lavinia was sipping coffee and looking quite deplorable, with her pretty dress covered in soot and bits of straw and a great tear in its skirt. Her hair had tumbled down too, giving her the look of a lost waif.

Radmer shook his head. 'There'll be a nurse with the ambulance, once we've seen them safely on their way, I'll take you home.'

She smoothed back a wisp of hair in an absent-minded fashion. 'You're coming home too?'

'I shall go over to the hospital when I've seen you indoors.'

Lavinia put her cup down. 'I'd like to come with you—that's if you don't mind. Just to be sure she's all right—and the babies.'

He raised his eyebrows. 'My dear girl, it's getting on for three o'clock in the morning.' He smiled at her kindly. 'Besides, what could you do? And I'll probably be there some time.'

She stooped to pick up the toddler who had wakened suddenly and burst into outraged tears. 'Yes, of course,' she answered in a colourless voice, 'how silly of me not to think of that.' She began wandering about the hall, the moppet against her shoulder, murmuring to it, not looking at Radmer at all.

The ambulance came almost immediately after that and she went and stood out of the way, in a corner with Mevrouw van de Platte, watching the mother and her children being expertly removed by two ambulance men and a pretty nurse, with Radmer quietly in charge of the whole undertaking, and presently, when he had bidden their kind hostess good-bye, she added her own thanks to his, wished the older lady good-bye in her turn, and went out to the car with him.

'You must be tired,' Radmer observed as they

went down the drive and into the road. 'Did you find the car difficult to handle?'

'Yes,' said Lavinia baldly, 'I did. At least, it wasn't the car, it was me—I've only ever driven an Austin 1100, and that was years ago.'

He grunted noncommittally and didn't speak again for quite some time, and then it was to make some remark about Peta and Sibby's return; it was very obvious that he didn't want to talk about the fire; which was a pity, for she longed, like a little girl, to be praised for her help. She swallowed tears and stared resolutely out of the window at the dark streets of Amstelveen. They would soon be home.

At the house he got out with her, opened the massive front door and followed her in, and when she said in a surprised voice: 'Oh, I thought you were going to the hospital,' he said with the faintest hint of impatience: 'I can hardly go like this—I'll change.'

Lavinia looked him over carefully. His clothes, at first glance, appeared to be ruined; filthy with stains of heaven knew what and grimy with soot and smoke, and there was a jagged tear in one trouser leg. She asked suddenly: 'You're not hurt?'

'Not in the least. We look a pretty pair, don't we?' He smiled briefly. 'Go to bed, Lavinia.'

She went towards the staircase, her bedraggled wrap trailing from one arm. At their foot she turned to encounter his hard stare. 'Good night, my dear, you were splendid.'

She didn't answer; she wanted to be hugged and fussed over and told she was the most wonderful and bravest girl in the world. She summoned up a smile and went slowly up the stairs, dragging her feet, sliding her hand along the polished balustrade. She was almost at the top when he spoke again, so quietly that she almost didn't hear him. His voice sounded as though the words had been dragged out of him. 'These last few hours have been the worst I have ever known—and I've only just realized it.'

She supposed him to be talking about the fire and the efforts he had made to rescue the farmer and his family; he must be tired... She said in a motherly little voice, meant to soothe: 'Yes—I was scared too, and I wasn't even in danger...'

Radmer had started towards the staircase, now he stopped to laugh so that Lavinia looked at him in bewilderment. She was on the point of asking him what was so funny when Mevrouw Pette, swathed in a dressing-gown and with her hair severely plaited, appeared on the landing above and leaned over the head of the stairs to stare down at them both, burst into speech and bear down upon Lavinia, whom she swept under a motherly wing and led towards her room, exchanging a rapid fire of question and answer with the professor as she did so.

Lavinia was tired and dispirited; it was pleasant to be fussed over, to have a bath run for her, to have her ruined gown removed with sympathetic tuts, and after a quick bath, to be tucked up in her vast bed like a small child. She drank the hot milk Mevrouw Pette insisted upon and went to sleep at once despite the kaleidoscope of events, nicely muddled with her tiredness, going on inside her head.

She woke to find Bep standing by her bed with a tray in her hands, and when she looked at the little bedside clock she saw to her astonishment that it was almost ten o'clock. She sat up, struggling to assemble her Dutch, and came out with: 'Late—I must get up.'

Bep smiled and shook her head, put the tray on Lavinia's lap and indicated the folded note propped against the coffee pot. It was a scrawl from Radmer, telling her simply that he would go straight from the hospital after he had finished his work there, to fetch Sibby and Peta; she could expect them all home for dinner, he hoped she would enjoy a quiet day, he was hers, R.

Lavinia had been looking forward to the drive to Noordwijk, for she had quickly gathered that Radmer had no intention of allowing her to infringe upon his work, and somehow he seemed to have very little leisure. It was obvious to her now that their two evenings out together had been in the nature of a sop to her acceptance without fuss of his plans for their wedding, and yet she had thought on the previous evening, while they had been dancing, that he was enjoying her company.

Wishful thinking, she told herself, drank the rest of her coffee, fed the toast to the birds on the balcony so that Mevrouw Pette would think that she had made a good breakfast, and got up. She would have to do something to take her mind off her problems, just for a little while. She didn't know how to handle the situation and panicking about it wouldn't help. One thing was certain; the quicker she got herself used to the manner of living Radmer expected of her, the better; she would have to learn to fill her days for herself and never take the sharing of his leisure for granted. She had the two girls, of course, and naturally there would be evenings out with his friends and family and some entertaining at home as well, when they would be together, but any vague hope which she had cherished that they might sometimes slip off together just for the sheer pleasure of each other's company could be scotched.

She dressed rapidly, snatched up her handbag and her lesson books, and after a short conversation with Mevrouw Pette, left the house. Her Dutch lesson would take care of the next hour and after that, she told herself, with a touch of defiance, she would go shopping.

Juffrouw de Waal was sharp with her; not only did she not know her lessons, she was decidedly distraite. She was sent on her way at the end of the hour, with a stern recommendation to apply herself to her Dutch verbs, and by way of penance, write a short essay on any subject she wished—in Dutch, of course. She agreed meekly to her teacher's views on her shortcomings, rather to that lady's surprise, and went out into the sunny streets. Five minutes' walk brought her to the shops and here she slowed her pace until her eye was caught by the sight of an extremely exclusive hair dressing salon. She went inside on an impulse and luckily for her the exquisite damsel at the reception desk felt sure that someone could be found to attend to her immediately and when she was asked to give her name, the damsel murmured: 'Oh, Mevrouw ter Bavinck,' rather as though she had introduced herself as the Queen of the Netherlands, and before she knew where she was, she had been whisked away to be attended by the proprietor himself, Monsieur Henri, who talked a great deal about the ter Bavinck family in a tone of reverence which greatly astonished her.

She emerged an hour later, considerably poorer, with her hair transformed from its usual simple style to an artless coiffure which looked simple but wasn't. Such a transformation deserved a new outfit; she spent a delightful half hour in La Bonneterie, emerging presently with a splendid collection of boxes and parcels, so that she was forced to get a taxi back to the house. Besides, she was very late for lunch, for it was long past one o'clock and she had told Mevrouw Pette that she would be back well before half past twelve.

The taxi driver was so kind as to carry her packages up to the door; Lavinia gathered them up in both arms, opened it with some difficulty and went inside.

Radmer was standing at his open study door, and at the expression on his face she faltered a little on her way across the hall. He looked tired; he looked furiously angry as well. She made for one of the marble-topped console tables in order to shed her purchases and he came to meet her, taking them from her and laying them down carefully, and when she stole another look at him, he didn't look angry at all, only tired.

He said blandly: 'I had expected you to be still in bed, sleeping off last night's exertions.' He smiled faintly. 'Have you had lunch?'

She flushed. 'No. I—I was shopping and I didn't

notice the time.' They entered the dining-room together and Bep, by some well-managed miracle, was already there, waiting to serve the soup. 'I didn't expect you to come home,' she went on coldly. 'From your note...'

He stared at her across the table. After a pause he said merely: 'I hope you had a good morning's shopping?'

She took a good drink of wine and felt it warm her cold inside. 'Yes, thank you. I spent a great deal of money.'

He was still staring at her and there was a gleam of amusement in his eyes now, although she didn't see it. Surely he would say something about her hair? It had looked quite different at the hairdressers, but all he said was: 'I'm sure you will have spent it to advantage. I'm sorry that pretty dress was ruined.'

'Oh, it's not ruined,' she told him earnestly. 'I'll have it cleaned and I can mend the tear quite easily. I'll send your dinner jacket to the cleaners too and see if they'll repair that tear in the leg...'

He answered her seriously although the gleam was decidedly more pronounced. 'Oh, I don't think I should bother about that—I've more than one suit, I believe, and why not buy another dress instead of—er—patching up the torn one?' He leaned over to re-fill her glass. 'If you need any more money, just say so.'

Was he annoyed because she had spent so much that morning? She went rather pink and said gruffly: 'I've a great deal of money left, thank you.'

He nodded rather vaguely and she asked him how the farmer and his wife were, and then, desperate for a nice neutral subject, enlarged on the weather. It was almost a relief when he said that he would have to be getting back to the hospital.

'I'll bring the girls back in good time,' he told her, and was gone before she had time to frame a careful request to go with him. Left alone, she reflected that perhaps it was a good thing that she had had no chance to say anything, for if he had wanted her to go with him, surely he would have said so. She wandered out of the dining-room and upstairs to her room, where her shopping had been laid out for her. It should have been great fun trying on the pretty things she had bought, but it wasn't; if Radmer was indifferent enough not to notice that her waist-length hair, instead of being pinned in a neat topknot, had been swathed round her head and the strands twisted and crossed high in front and pinned by a handsome tortoiseshell comb, he certainly wouldn't notice what clothes she wore. She took a close look at her reflection now and wondered if she would ever be able to dress her hair herself—probably not, but at least she would leave it as it was until Sibendina and Peta came home to admire it; she would wear one of her new dresses too. She decided on a silver grey silk jersey smock with an important colour and very full sleeves caught into deep cuffs. It was floor-length and she considered that it was exactly the sort of garment a stepmother might be expected to wear. Studying it in the mirror, she came to the erroneous conclusion that it added dignity to her appearance and made her look much older. In fact, it did nothing of the sort—indeed, she looked younger if anything, and positively pretty.

She got back into a cotton dress finally and took the dogs out into the park. The lovely summer day had become a little overcast and as she turned for home with Dong and Pobble at her heels, she could see black clouds massing over the rooftops. There was going to be a storm, and she hated them; it wouldn't be quite so bad if she were back home with Mevrouw Pette and Bep in the kitchen. She put the dogs on their leads and hurried. They gained the porch, very out of breath as the first slow drops of rain fell.

Lavinia had her solitary tea sitting with her back to the enormous windows, and tried not to flinch at each flash of lightning, and the dogs, quite as cowardly as she, pressed themselves close to her. But presently the storm blew over, leaving a downpour of rain, and she got out her lesson books and applied herself to her homework until it was time to go and change her dress. She took a long time over this; even so, there was still plenty of time before Radmer and the girls would arrive. She filled it in by inspecting the table in the diningroom. While she was there Mevrouw Pette came in, and together they admired the stiffly starched linen, the polished silver and sparkling glass. Between them they had concocted a festive menu too, and Lavinia, glad to have something to do, accompanied the housekeeper back to the kitchen to sample the delicacies prepared in honour of the girls' homecoming.

It was pleasant in the kitchen, warm and fragrant with the smell of cooking, and the copper pans on the wall glowed cosily and it was nice when its occupants complimented her upon her appearance, even Ton, who came in each day to help, a good hard-working girl but hardly talkative, managed to tell her that she looked pretty. Lavinia went back upstairs sparkling with their praise, and the sparkle was still there a few minutes later when the front door was flung open and hurrying feet across the hall heralded the family's return. The girls came in together, calling 'Lavinia!' at the tops of their voices, to stop and stare at her waiting for them in the centre of the drawing-room. 'Gosh, you look absolutely gorgeous!' cried Peta. 'You've done something to your hair, and look at that wizard dress...'

'Why, you're pretty,' declared Sibby with the candour of youth. 'You always are,' she added hastily, 'but you know what I mean.'

The pair of them fell upon her, hugging and kissing her in a fashion to warm her heart although she cried laughingly: 'Oh, darlings, do take care of my hair!'

They let her go then, still holding her hands, turning and twisting her from side to side, admiring every aspect of her person, talking and giggling until Sibby cried: 'Papa, doesn't Lavinia look absolutely super? No wonder you wanted to marry her—and don't you just love the way her hair is done?'

Lavinia hadn't known that he was in the room. She said too quickly: 'Dinner's all ready—hadn't you two better go upstairs and wash your hands?' She smiled rather blindly at them and then turned round to face him. 'I do hope you had a pleasant drive and that your parents are well,' she observed cheerfully; she sounded like a hostess, anxious to please, and the two girls exchanged puzzled glances as they went from the room.

He poured their drinks with a brief: 'Yes, thanks,' but when he brought her glass over, he remarked ruefully: 'I should have said something about the hair, shouldn't I? I'm sorry, I did notice it, you know. I told you that I had become clumsy with women, didn't I? Please forgive me. And your dress is very pretty.'

Lavinia thanked him quietly and took a heartening sip of her sherry; she felt that she needed it. Perhaps when the girls had gone to bed, she should have a talk with him; try and get back on to the old friendly footing which somehow they had lost. On the other hand, he was probably tired and the awkwardness she felt between them was due to that. She finished her sherry and asked for another, and when he handed it to her he said with a twinkle: 'Dutchman's courage, Lavinia?'

Of course he thought that she was nervous because the girls had come back; quite likely he imagined that she had dressed up and had her hair done with the same reason in mind. She smiled at him and lied cheerfully: 'Yes, I think I need it— I'm nervous, isn't it silly? though I'll get over it. It's lovely to have them here, isn't it?'

Radmer's voice was bland. 'Delightful,' he agreed, and added lightly: 'And such a weight off my shoulders, I shall be able to catch up on my reading without feeling guilty of leaving Sibendina alone.' He put down his glass. 'How do you like the idea of Peta having Dutch lessons with Juffrouw de Waal? Not with you, of course, and I thought it might be a good idea if she had lessons in Dutch history and geography, and as soon as she has a smattering of Dutch, she could go to Sibby's school—I'm sure they will take her. Do you suppose she would like that?'

Lavinia lifted a grateful face to him. 'Oh, Radmer, how kind you are—I'm sure she'll love it. Have you asked her?'

He looked surprised. 'Well, no—I hadn't spoken to you about it, my dear.'

She wished most fervently that she was his dear. 'Is there anything I can do to save your time?' she asked, and when he shook his head, she repeated: 'You've been more than kind,' and then before she could stop herself because the sherry was doing its work: 'Why didn't you want me to go with you to Noordwijk?'

He was standing close to her, watching her. Now he frowned. 'I'm not sure,' he told her. 'I...' Whatever he had been about to say was cut short by the entry of the two girls and they all went in to dinner.

The meal was a gay one, with a great deal of laughing and talking, and if Lavinia was a little quieter than the others, no one seemed to notice.

They made plans later, sitting in the drawing-room while Lavinia poured the coffee, and Peta immediately professed the greatest satisfaction with the plan for her to have lessons with Juffrouw de Waal; she was to join Sibby's tennis club too, and go swimming whenever she wished, and when Radmer disclosed his plans for sending her to Sibby's school just as soon as she had mastered a little Dutch, she was in transports of delight.

'And now what about going to bed?' he wanted to know, cutting her thanks short. 'Sibby has to go to school in the morning and I suggest that you go with Lavinia, Peta, and meet Juffrouw de Waal.'

They said good night, embracing Lavinia first and then going to kiss Radmer. It was Peta who observed bracingly: 'You mustn't be shy about kissing Lavinia, you know, while we're here—we shan't mind at all.' She continued reflectively: 'You didn't when we came home this evening.'

It was Sibendina who unconsciously saved the situation by remarking: 'Well, they're only just married, you know, I expect they like to be alone. Don't you, Papa?'

'Oh, decidedly,' agreed the professor mildly. 'And now bed, my dears.'

They went, giggling and talking still, up the stairs, and when their voices could no longer be heard, Lavinia got up too. 'Well, I think I'll go to bed as well,' she told him. 'I daresay you want the house quiet so that you can read in peace.'

'Good lord, did I say that?' he asked her, and when she laughed, 'You're a very nice girl, Lavinia,' He walked to the door with her and opened it, but when she made to pass him, he put out a sudden hand and caught her by the shoulder.

'We're quite alone,' he said lightly. 'We'd better do as Sibby suggested.'

He bent to kiss her, a brief salute on one cheek, and then to her utter surprise, a quite rough kiss on her mouth. He let her go at once and she flew away, up the staircase and into her room before she really knew what she was doing. Undressing, she told herself that she had behaved in the stupidest fashion; like a silly schoolgirl. She should have made a graceful little joke about it, instead of tearing off in that way. He must think her a complete fool. She got into bed, determined that it wouldn't happen again; she would be careful to keep such incidents as lighthearted as possible, if ever they should occur again. She closed her eyes resolutely upon this resolve, although her last thought before she slept was that being kissed in that fashion was decidedly interesting, even if he had intended it as a joke.

CHAPTER EIGHT

IT WAS A simple matter to slip into the well-ordered way of living which Radmer's household enjoyed. Lavinia, aided by the kindly Mevrouw Pette, took upon herself those household tasks which the housekeeper considered were suitable for the lady of the house, although in actual fact they took up very little of her time, but she worked for hours over her Dutch lessons and she was always home when the girls got back at lunchtime, and never failed to be sitting by the tea tray when they came home in the afternoon. Of Radmer she saw very little. True, they breakfasted together, but then so did the girls, and conversation, such as it was, was general. He was always the first to leave the table, and perhaps because of what Peta had said, he never neglected to come round the table and bend to kiss her cheek, and if Sibby and Peta were with her when he got back in the evenings, he repeated this, while she, for her part, greeted him with a welcoming smile and a few wifely inquiries as to how his day had gone. Very rarely he came home for lunch, although he never went out in the evenings, retiring after a decent interval to his study,

176

so that before very long Lavinia was forced to the conclusion that he was avoiding her as often as he could.

On one or two occasions they had dined out with friends and they all paid regular visits to Noordwijk, but the opportunity to talk to him, even get to know him better, was non-existent. And yet, on the rare occasions when they were together, he appeared to take pleasure in her being with him, and from every other aspect she supposed that their marriage was a success, for Sibby was deeply fond of her already and even though she regarded her more as an elder sister than a stepmother, she confided in her to an extent which proved how much in need she had been for an older and wiser head with which to share her youthful problems.

Peta was happy too. Lavinia had never seen her so carefree and content, treating Radmer like a big brother and yet quite obviously regarding him as the head of the household to be obeyed, as well as the one to go to when in trouble.

The house had taken on a new air, too. It had always been beautifully managed by Mevrouw Pette, but now Lavinia was slowly setting her own mark upon it; arranging great bowls of flowers in every room, bearing home baskets of plants from the flower market and bedding them in great masses of colour in the small garden. She had taken over the conservatory too, buying new lounge chairs and a hammock seat which was the delight of the girls, and attending with loving care to a vine she had planted there. She did these things gradually and by the end of a month she had made a niche for herself, so that, while not absolutely essential to the life of the house, she certainly contributed to its well-being. Her Dutch was making strides too, and now that Peta was having many more lessons than she herself was, it was an incentive to work even harder at her books. And as for Radmer, he seemed content enough and at week-ends at least, quite prepared to take them out and about, but there had been no more tête-à-tête dinners, and as the days slipped by, Lavinia resigned herself to the fact that there probably never would be again.

They were to go to Friesland for a short holiday in August; the professor had a yacht which he kept at Sneek and they would go sailing for a good deal of the time, as well as touring Friesland. Lavinia, collecting a suitable wardrobe with the help of Sibby, who knew all about life on board a boat, hoped that she would quickly pick up all the salient points about sailing. She had mentioned, rather diffidently, that she didn't know one end of a boat from the other, but Radmer had only laughed and told her that she would soon learn.

They set off one Saturday, in a brilliant morning which promised to become hot later in the day, and drove straight to the ter Bavinck estate, where Juffrouw Hengsma was waiting for them, and this time Lavinia was able to address her in Dutch, which pleased her mightily and made Radmer laugh.

'You are making progress, Lavinia,' he observed. 'Now you must learn the Friesian language, because Juffrouw Hengsma prefers to speak that.' He had spoken to her in Dutch too, to her secret delight, and she answered him haltingly in that tongue, feeling that sharing his language was a small link between them.

They had coffee together before they went to their rooms to unpack and then meet again to wander round the house and grounds. Radmer ran a small stable and naturally enough they spent a good deal of time there, and when he offered to teach Peta to ride, she flung her arms round his neck. 'You really are a darling!' she declared. 'I do hope there'll be someone like you for me when I grow up.'

He laughed gently at her and tweaked her ear. 'I'll make a point of finding just the right one,' he assured her. 'Sibby has already told me whom she intends marrying, so I'll only have you to worry about.'

He flung an arm round Sibby's shoulders. 'Sibby has made a very wise choice, too,' he added, and she grinned widely.

'I don't mind Lavinia and Peta knowing,' she told him, and tucked an arm into Lavinia's. 'He's a student at St Jorus, but I've known him for years, ever since I was a baby. Peta, who do you want to marry?'

'I've just said—someone like Radmer, and we'll have dozens of babies and they'll grow up very clever and be doctors...' She looked at Lavinia. 'Are you going to have some babies, Lavinia?'

Lavinia felt her cheeks redden, although she said airily enough: 'There's certainly heaps of room for them, isn't there? And wouldn't this be a gorgeous place for their holidays? Did you like coming here when you were a little girl, Sibby?'

She only half listened to Sibby's reply. She was dreaming, just for a few delightful moments, of a carload of little boys, blue-eyed and flaxen-haired like their father, and a sprinkling of little girls, much prettier than their mother, tumbling around, laughing and shouting. She blinked the dream away and asked Radmer when he intended to go sailing.

The marvellous weather held. They spent long, lazy days swimming in the pool in one corner of the grounds, playing tennis on the court behind the house, or just sitting and doing nothing. Lavinia felt herself unwinding slowly so that she was able to think of the future, if not through rose-coloured spectacles, at least with a degree of optimism.

'I shall get fat,' she worried out loud as they lounged on the terrace after breakfast. 'I don't do anything...'

Radmer looked up from his newspaper and allowed his gaze to sweep over her. 'Never fat—curvaceous is the word, I believe. It suits you—besides, you're hardly idle; you swim and play tennis, and now you're not frightened any more on Juno, we shall have you galloping in all directions before we go back to Amsterdam.' He stood up slowly. 'I've some telephoning to do, then we'll drive over to Sneek and take a look at the yacht.'

She watched him go, her heart in her eyes, and in turn she was watched by Peta and Sibby. When he had rounded the corner of the house Sibby spoke: 'You are happy, aren't you, Lavinia?' She sounded anxious, so that Lavinia said at once and warmly: 'Oh, my dear—yes. Why do you ask?'

It was Peta who joined in. 'We've noticed—you never kiss each other or—or hold hands, do you? Oh, I know Radmer pecks your cheek twice a day—I don't mean that—I mean...' she hesitated. 'Well, we expected you'd be... You act like good friends.'

'We are good friends, my dears,' said Lavinia steadily. 'There are lots of ways of loving people, you know, and perhaps you forget that your papa—Radmer—is a busy man. He comes home tired. Besides, his work is more important to him than anything else.' She looked across at Sibendina and smiled. 'That doesn't mean you, Sibby.'

And because the girls looked so unhappy still, she went on gaily: 'How about getting ready?' She looked down at her nicely tanned person. 'Ought I to wear slacks?'

They decided that she should and they all went upstairs, laughing together, so that Lavinia was quite reassured that Sibby's little outburst had been quite forgotten.

She was the last down, and she hadn't known that they would all be waiting for her in the hall. She had put on the pale blue denim slacks and an Indian cotton shirt which matched them exactly, and her hair she had brushed back, plaited into a waist-long rope and tied with a blue ribbon. She looked, she had considered, exactly right for a day's sailing.

It was therefore a little disconcerting to hear Sibby's cry of: 'Oh, smashing, Lavinia, and very sexy too—isn't she, Peta?'

'Oh, rather,' echoed Peta. 'Hey, Radmer, what do you think...?'

But Lavinia interrupted her, studying herself worriedly. 'But I thought it was exactly right…'

Radmer had been bending over the straps of the picnic basket, but he had straightened up to watch Lavinia come down the stairs. His blue eyes, very bright under their heavy lids, met hers. 'It's exactly right,' he told her, and his placid voice set her doubts at rest at once, so that, quite happy again, she skipped down the last stair or two, declaring that she must just have a word with Juffrouw Hengsma before they went. She was pleased that Radmer found her appearance quite normal, although a small, sneaking wish that he could have found her sexy too persisted at the back of her mind. She dispelled it sternly; of course he wouldn't, and come to think of it, she wasn't.

She felt that she had further proof of this when they got into the car, for Radmer suggested in the nicest possible way that Sibby might like to sit in front with him, which meant that Lavinia shared the back seat with Peta and the dogs. She listened to Sibby's happy chatter, and told herself it was foolish of her to feel hurt; Sibby had as much right to sit beside Radmer as she had—besides, it had seemed to her just lately that he had become somehow remote, retreating behind a friendly front which while pleasant enough, kept her at arms' length. Was he regretting their marriage already, and if he were, what had she done or not done to make him feel that way?

She made up her mind to discover what it was. Perhaps she had been spending too much? There had been clothes, more than she needed, she thought guiltily, and although Radmer invariably complimented her when she appeared in something new, he might be annoyed at her extravagance, and then there had been clothes for the girls, the new furniture for the conservatory, the flowers she delighted in buying, her lessons, Peta's lessons... He had told her not to worry about money, but she had no idea how much of it he had. She had better ask him at the first opportunity and have a sensible talk at the same time before the constraint between them had built itself up into an insurmountable barrier.

Having come to this decision, she sensibly decided to forget about it for the time being, and applied herself to the pleasant task of answering the girls' excited babble. An opportunity would present itself sooner or later, she felt sure.

Sooner, as it turned out. They had boarded the *Mimi* at Sneek, and Lavinia had been quite overcome by the size and comfort of her. Sibby had taken her and Peta on a tour of inspection while Radmer got the yacht ready to sail, and she had admired the cabins and the galley and all the mod cons which she had never expected to find. It was all simply lovely. She went back on deck and told him so, a little breathless with the excitement of it all, that the *Mimi* was the most marvellous boat she had ever thought to see, and he had thanked her gravely. 'And later on,' he had added, 'when we've had lunch, the girls can sunbathe and I'll give you your first lesson in sailing her.'

They had set sail then, using the *Mimi*'s engine to travel down the canal which took them to Sneek-emeer, and once there, they had bowled along before a stiff breeze until the girls clamoured for their lunch, when they tied up to a small, broken-down jetty on the further bank of the lake and eaten their sandwiches and fruit. The younger members of the party had packed up afterwards while Lavinia was shown how to sail the yacht out into the lake again. She managed rather well; almost stammering with pleased surprise at herself, she cried: 'I did it—isn't it a marvellous feeling? May I carry on for a while?' She looked around her; there were plenty of other boats about, but none very near. 'I shan't bump into anything, shall I?'

Radmer was lounging beside her, apparently content to let her take the yacht where she wished. 'Not at the moment. Set a course for that clump of trees at the end of the lake; there's a canal close by which leads to a charming stretch of water.'

Peta and Sibby had stretched themselves out in the bows, lying on their stomachs, half asleep. There was only the gentle splash of water around them and the faint sounds from the shore mingling in with the bird cries. Very peaceful, thought Lavinia, and closed her eyes to enjoy it all better. But only for a second; she felt Radmer's hand clamp down on hers and his voice, half laughing, said: 'Hey, you can't sail a boat with your eyes shut!' His blue eyes surveyed hers. 'Would you like to sunbathe too?'

She was very conscious of his hand, still holding hers fast. 'No—no, I'd like to talk, if you don't mind.'

He was lighting his pipe, but he paused to look at her. 'Of course we can talk, dear girl. What about?'

She met his gaze bravely. 'You and me—us. It's a little awkward and I daresay I'll get a bit muddled, only if we don't talk about it now it'll only get worse.' She paused, but he said nothing, looking at her now with the faintest of smiles. 'You see, we were friends, weren't we? I mean before we married, and afterwards too, and I thought it was going to be all right—we both knew what it was going to be like, didn't we? Only it's not turning out...I thought we were getting on rather well; I tried to keep out of your way as much as I could—I still do, for you did tell me that your work was more important to you than anything else and I—I can understand that, and I can understand you not wanting to talk about your wife—you must have loved her very much, even if…so it's natural for you to…' She came to a stop, finding it much harder to explain than she had imagined it would be. 'I told you it would be muddled,' she said crabbily.

He had taken his hand away. Now he put it back again in an absent-minded manner, but he said nothing, so that after a moment she felt forced to go on. 'I wondered if I'd been spending too much money…' and stopped at his laugh.

'Lavinia, did I not tell you not to worry about money? You could buy a dozen dresses at a time if you had a mind to do so. I think you have been very careful in your spending—and there is not the least need of that.'

She looked ahead of her. 'Are you very rich?' she asked.

'Very. You see, I have money of my own—I inherited it from my grandparents—a great deal of money, Lavinia, and besides that, I make a good living at my work.'

'Oh, well, it isn't that, is it?' She smiled at him with relief. 'That's one thing settled. So it must be your wife…'

He gave her a long searching look from under his heavy lids. 'Are you not my wife, my dear?'

She frowned at him. 'Yes, of course I am, but you know very well what I mean.' She rushed on, anxious to say what she intended as quickly as possible. 'You see, now we're married, perhaps you feel that I'm trying…that is, I do want you to understand that I'll never come between you and her.' Her voice became rather high and very earnest. 'I wouldn't want to anyway.'

'Shall we be quite blunt?' His voice was bland. 'What you are trying to say, in carefully muffled-up ladylike phrases, is that you have no wish to—er—form a deeper relationship with me and that any fears I had on that score may be safely put at rest and we can be friends again. Is that not the gist of the matter? Well, Lavinia,' he spoke with deliberation, 'let me set your mind at rest; you could never come between me and Helga.'

Lavinia heard these words with a sinking heart. She had said what she had wanted to say, true enough, but his answer, which should have satisfied her, had only served to make her wish to burst into tears. But she did know where she stood now—any faint hopes she might have been cherishing that he might fall in love with her could be killed off once and for all. She let out a long sigh, quite unconscious of doing so, and slamming a mental lid down on the conversation exclaimed: 'Oh, look, we're almost at the end of the lake. Shall I hand over to you now?'

She was looking away from him as she spoke, studying the scenery with eyes which really saw none of it, so that she failed to see the expression on her companion's face.

Peta came to take her place soon afterwards and she went and lay down close to Sibendina, letting the sun warm her, although she felt that the coldness inside her would never go away again.

They had another few days of sailing before they returned to Amsterdam, and although Radmer treated her with an easy-going friendliness and consideration, Lavinia couldn't help but notice that he avoided being alone with her, so although she was sorry to leave the lovely old house and the simple pleasures of their holiday, she was relieved to be involved once more in the routine of their Amsterdam home. Sibendina was still on holiday, and although Peta went each day to Juffrouw de Waal, she was free for a good deal of the day. The three of them went out a good deal together, exploring the city, and in the evenings Radmer, putting aside his work for the time being, took them to the Concertgebouw, the Stadsschouwburg for the opera, and on a tour of the city's canals after dark. He was an excellent escort, she discovered, for he knew the city well and took pains to tell her as much about it as possible. They went to den Haag too, to dine out and visit the Koninklijke Schouwburg. The season was over, but although the ballet was finished, there were plays—in Dutch, which Radmer pointed out were very good for Lavinia and Peta.

They went to Delft, to watch the military tattoo. Lavinia had never been out so much in her life before, nor, for that matter, had she been able to indulge her taste in clothes to such an extent. She should have been very happy, and she tried hard to present a bright face to the world while she saw Radmer becoming increasingly remote—if only he wasn't so nice, she thought desperately, if only there was a good reason to have a quarrel—it might clear the air. But he remained kind, good-natured, and despite his preoccupation with his work, careful that she should want for nothing. All the same, they were almost never alone, and on the two occasions when the two girls had gone to bed, leaving them sitting together in the drawing-room, Radmer had excused himself within a very few minutes on the grounds of work to be done, and after that second time Lavinia had taken care to follow the girls upstairs, to sit lonely in her room with her unhappy thoughts.

It was a morning shortly after this, as she faced

him across the breakfast table before the girls got down, that he said casually: 'I've ordered a Mini for you, Lavinia. I thought you might like a car of your own—you've proved yourself a good driver, so I don't need to worry on that score, but I'm afraid you will have to wait several weeks for it to be delivered.'

She had picked up the coffee pot, but now she set it down again. 'For me?' she asked. 'A car for me? How very kind of you, Radmer—thank you very much—how absolutely super! I'll have to get a licence, won't I?' She smiled with delight. 'I'll be able to visit your mother...'

He was buttering toast and didn't look at her. 'You get on well with her?'

'Oh, yes, we're already the best of friends. She calls here quite often, you know—when she comes to Amsterdam to shop. She's going to take me to Bergen-op-Zoom one day soon, to visit your sister.'

He frowned. 'Something I should have done already.'

She had picked up the coffee pot once more. 'Why should you? You're at St Jorus all day and almost every day,' she answered quietly. She smiled at him as she spoke and was astonished at the expression on his face—Rage? Exasperation? She wondered which; she had always supposed him to be an even-tempered man, but now suddenly she wasn't sure. The look had gone so quickly, though, that she was left wondering if she had imagined it, and his face was as bland as his voice. 'That is so, my dear—you don't object?'

She buttered a roll. 'You said once that I was a sensible girl and that my feet were planted firmly on the ground. They still are, Radmer.'

Their eyes met and he made an impatient gesture. 'Did I really say that?' he wanted to know, and added inexplicably: 'But in another world.'

An odd remark which she would have challenged if the girls hadn't come in at that moment.

It was Sibendina who remarked, after they had exchanged good mornings: 'You look awfully pleased with yourself, Lavinia. Has Papa given you a diamond coronet?'

'Oh, much nicer than that,' said Lavinia, stifling an ungrateful wish that his gift had indeed been some extravagant trifle to adorn her commonplace person. 'A car—a Mini.'

The two of them chorused their pleasure and Sibby wanted to know when she would have one too.

'When you're eighteen, *liefje*,' her father declared firmly. 'And Peta too, of course.'

This statement was met with cries of delight and a sudden surging of the pair of them from their places at table, to hug him. He bore their onslaught with fortitude, looking at Lavinia over their heads with a faintly mocking smile which caused her to pinken deeply; the difference between the girls' rapturous thanks and her own staid gratitude was only too well marked. Should she have leapt to her feet and rushed round the table and hugged him too? She wondered what he would have done if she had. She busied herself with the coffee cups and didn't look at him again, not until she raised startled eyes to his, when, Peta and Sibby once more settled in their chairs, he remarked: 'I've ordered another car too, though we shall have to wait a long time for it. It's the new Rolls-Royce—the Camargue.'

The girls burst into excited chatter, but he took no notice of them, looking down the table at Lavinia, her mouth a little open with surprise. 'You'll like that, Lavinia?'

'Like it?' she managed. 'It'll be out of this world! But won't it be too big?'

'Not a bit of it—just right for holidays with the four of us—besides, I take up a lot of room. You'll look nice sitting in a Rolls, my dear.' He got up from the table. 'I shall be late home this evening; I have to go to Utrecht to give a lecture. I'll leave there about six o'clock, I expect, and get here half an hour later.' He kissed Sibby good-bye and then

Peta, and last of all Lavinia, a brief peck on her cheek. 'Unless, of course,' he added smoothly, 'I meet any old friends who want me to spend the evening with them.'

'Old friends?' Sibby giggled. 'Lady friends, Papa?'

'That's telling,' he grinned at her, and a moment later the front door closed behind him.

Lavinia had a busy day before her; her usual lesson with Juffrouw de Waal, some shopping to do for Sibby, who was going back to school the next day, and some books to buy for Peta's lessons. Besides, her mother-in-law was coming to have coffee with her and in the afternoon she had promised to go to the hospital to Zuster Smid's tea party, given in honour of Neeltje's birthday. She bustled around, seeing the girls off for a walk with the dogs, arranging lunch with Mevrouw Pette and arranging the flowers she had bought from the nice old man who came past the door each week with his barrow. She was running downstairs after tidying herself at the conclusion of these house-wifely exertions, when Mevrouw ter Bavinck was admitted, and the two ladies went at once to the sitting-room, gossiping happily about nothing in particular, pleased to be in each other's company.

It was after they had been seated for ten minutes or so and the first cups of coffee had been drunk that Mevrouw ter Bavinck inquired: 'Well, Lavinia, how do you like being married to Radmer?'

Lavinia cast her companion a startled glance, wondering why on earth she should ask such a question. 'Very much,' she said at length.

'And has he told you about Helga?'

'No—I don't think he intends to.'

Her companion blinked at her. 'No? And do you not wish to know?'

'Very much, but I wouldn't dream of asking him.'

The older woman put her cup and saucer down on the table beside her. 'Radmer has led a solitary life for a good many years now, and it is all a long time ago—all the same, I find it strange that he hasn't explained...'

Lavinia stirred uncomfortably. 'Perhaps he can't bear to talk about her—he must have loved her very much.' She didn't look up. 'Oh, I know—at least I heard at the hospital that she was—was rather frivolous...'

She was cut short abruptly. 'Loved her?' questioned her mother-in-law. 'My dear child, after the first few months he had no feeling for her at all. She was quite unfitted to be his—any man's wife, but because she was expecting Sibby by then, he looked after her and to the outside world at least, they were happily married. Perhaps Radmer

thought that when the baby was born, they might
be able to patch things up again, but it was actually
worse. She had not wanted Sibby in the first place,
and once she was born she was left to a nurse and
Helga went back to her own way of living, and
although Radmer no longer loved her, he had
Sibby to consider. When Helga was killed—and I
will leave him to tell you about the accident—he
told me that he would never allow himself to love
a woman again, and at the time he meant it. Then
you came along, my dear, and everything was
changed.'

She beamed at Lavinia, who smiled back with
an effort. As far as she could see, nothing was
changed. Radmer lived in a world of his own making, content with it, too, not needing her or her
love, only a sensible young woman who would
mother his daughter and order his household. She
said now: 'That is very sad. What does Sibby think
of it?'

'It was explained to her that her mother died in
an accident when she was visiting a friend, and as
she cannot remember her at all, it has never mattered to her very much. She loves her father very
much, you will have seen that for yourself, and he
has done his best to be father and mother to her,
although I believe that you will make her an excellent mother, Lavinia—she loves you already,

you know. The dear child goes back to school to-morrow, does she not?'

They talked of other things after that, and presently the elder lady went off to do her shopping and Lavinia was left to do her own small chores while she mulled over what her mother-in-law had told her. She would have to get used to the idea of Radmer not loving Helga, although that fact made it clearer than ever why he had chosen to marry herself. He must have felt quite safe in marrying her, knowing that he had not a spark of love for her. The idea of falling in love with her must have been so remote to him that it would have been laughable.

She did her shopping in a sour state of mind and for the first time found Sibby's and Peta's chatter at lunch almost more than she could bear, but they went off arm-in-arm to play tennis at last, and Lavinia was able to indulge her desire to be alone and think. It was only a pity that after a few fruitless minutes she discovered that her rather woolly thoughts were of no value to her at all, and she had no idea as to how she could charm Radmer into loving her. She gave up and took the dogs out.

Six o'clock came and went and there was no sign of Radmer, an hour later the three of them sat down to dinner, and Lavinia did her best to check the girls' uneasiness. She was uneasy herself, but perhaps not for the same reasons as they; she remembered only too clearly what he had said about spending the evening with old friends, and he hadn't really denied it when Sibby had teased him about going out with a lady friend. Perhaps he had already arranged to meet her. He talked cheerfully to her two companions while her imagination ran riot, providing her with an image of some strikingly beautiful girl, superbly dressed and loaded with charm—the type men fell for...

The evening passed emptily and at nine o'clock the girls, at her suggestion, went to bed.

'I'll stay up,' she told them bracingly. 'Probably your papa has met old friends after all, Sibby.'

'Then why didn't he telephone?' demanded his daughter.

'Oh, darling, probably there wasn't a telephone handy.' It was a silly remark; Radmer, if he had wanted to telephone, would have found the means of doing so. But it contented Sibby, who gave her an affectionate kiss and went off to bed with Peta.

The bracket clock had chimed eleven o'clock in its small silvery voice when Lavinia went down to the kitchen. Bep had already gone to bed, Mevrouw Pette was sitting at the table, knitting. He looked up as Lavinia went in and said: 'The professor is late, Mevrouw.'

Lavinia answered in her careful, slow Dutch.

'Yes, I'll stay up, Mevrouw Pette, you go to bed. Perhaps you would leave some coffee ready?' She said good night and went back upstairs into the quiet room, where she sat down on one of the enormous sofas, a dog on either side of her. The house was still now, and the square outside was silent. She sat doing nothing, not thinking, watching the hands of the clock creep round its face. It was almost two o'clock when she fell asleep, still sitting bolt upright, the dogs' heads on her lap.

She wakened from an uneasy nap to hear the gentle click of the front door lock. Radmer was home. Lavinia's eyes flew to the clock's face; its delicately wrought hands stood at twenty minutes to three in the morning. She had been sitting there for simply hours. Rage and relief and love churned together inside her as she got off the sofa and erupted into one vast surge of feelings which manifested themselves in a cross, wifely voice. 'Where have you been?' she demanded in a loud whisper as she sped across the hall, quite forgetting that she had been weeping and that her face was puffy and stained with tears.

Radmer had given her a penetrating look as she spoke, not missing the tears or the sharp anxious voice on her white, tired face. If she had been nearer to him and the light had been brighter, she might have seen the sudden gleam in his eyes, very much at variance with his calm face.

He said now, as meekly as any husband would: 'I got held up, dear girl.'

Lavinia was so angry that she didn't wait for him to continue. 'You've been spending the evening with your old friends, I suppose,' she declared in a waspish whisper, 'not that I can blame you; you married me because I was sensible, not because I was good company...' She drew a deep breath and went on, anxious only to have her say, and not bothering about the consequences. 'Was she good fun, or shouldn't I ask that?' She paused, gave a snort of sheer temper and went on: 'I'm being vulgar, aren't I? and I'm quite enjoying it! Just to say what I...' She stopped, choked a little and went on in a quite different voice: 'I beg your pardon, Radmer, you look very tired, though I don't suppose that matters to you if you enjoyed yourself.' She wanted to giggle and cry at the same time, and it cost her quite an effort to say quietly: 'There's coffee in the kitchen, shall I fetch you some?'

He shook his head. 'No, thank you. Go to bed, Lavinia.' He spoke quietly and she knew that he was angry. She turned on her heel without another word and went upstairs to her room.

CHAPTER NINE

LAVINIA WAS LATE for breakfast, for after tossing and turning until the sky was light, she had fallen into a heavy sleep and wakened only when she had heard Sibby and Peta laughing and talking their way downstairs.

Radmer was reading his newspaper when she entered the dining-room, but he got up, wishing her good morning as he did so, pulled the bell-rope for more coffee, and sat himself down again. The girls greeted her with rather more animation, and then seeing her swollen eyelids and peaky face, demanded to know if she was feeling well. 'Not that I am surprised that you look as you do,' explained Sibby, 'for you must have been greatly upset when Papa came home and told you about the accident.'

'Accident? What accident?' Lavinia looked at them in turn, their faces expressing nothing but concern and astonishment. Radmer, invisible behind his paper, had apparently not been listening.

'But, Lavinia, you must have seen Papa when he came home...?'

'I dozed off in the drawing-room, I hadn't gone to bed. Radmer?'

The newspaper was lowered and his blue eyes, very calm, met hers. His bland: 'Yes, my dear?' was all that a wife could have wished for, but she almost snapped at him: 'You didn't tell me what happened? Were you hurt?'

'You were tired, Lavinia.' He smiled kindly. 'You shouldn't have stayed up for me, my dear.'

She wished irritably that he would stop calling her his dear when she wasn't anything of the sort. 'Yes—well, now I'd like to know.'

Before he could reply, Sibendina and Peta chorused together: 'There was a pile-up on the Utrecht motorway—it was on the news this morning, we heard it while we were dressing—and Papa stopped to help.'

'What a pair of gossips you are,' Radmer interpolated mildly. 'Suppose you go and get ready to go to school?'

They went, grumbling a little. Lavinia heard them going upstairs to their rooms, and when she could no longer hear their voices, she asked crossly: 'And why didn't you tell me? You let me say all those things about—about…you could have stopped me…'

'And then you wouldn't have said them,' he

pointed out reasonably, 'only thought them to
yourself. At least you have been honest.'

'I wasn't—I'm not.' Her voice, despite her best
efforts to remain calm, had become a good deal
higher. 'Anyone would suppose that you had done
it deliberately so that I should say all the...' She
stopped, because he wasn't looking at her, but over
her shoulder, towards the door, and when she
turned her head to look, there were the two girls,
standing silently, watching them. She wondered if
they had been there long.

But Radmer was smiling at them and he spoke
easily, just as though they had been enjoying a
pleasant conversation. 'I'll give you a lift,' he told
them, 'and drop you off at the end of the street;
Peta can walk round to Juffrouw de Waal from
there.'

He wished Lavinia a cheerful *'Tot ziens'* and a
few minutes later she heard the three of them leave
the house, the two girls chattering happily. Probably, she told herself uneasily, they hadn't heard
anything—Radmer would have seen them the moment they reached the door.

He came home at teatime—a great pity, for Lavinia, with the whole day in which to indulge in
self-pity, was spoiling for a quarrel, but as he
brought the girls with him, there was nothing she
could do but turn a cool cheek to his equally cool

kiss, inquire as to his day, and then join in the
schoolgirl high spirits of Peta and Sibendina, both
of whom had a great deal to say for themselves.
They looked at her curiously once or twice, for in
her efforts to be bright and gay, she only succeeded
in talking much too much and laughing a great deal
too often.

Nobody mentioned the traffic pile-up of the previous evening. Lavinia, who had struggled with little success to read about it in the newspapers, had
actually started out to enlist Juffrouw de Waal's
help in the matter, but on the point of doing so,
she remembered that this was one of the days when
Peta would be there with the teacher until teatime.
And what would the pair of them think if she were
to burst in, demanding to know about something
which any husband, in normal circumstances,
would have told his wife the moment he opened
his own front door?

Presently the girls went away to do their homework together in the small sitting-room on the first
floor, and as Radmer got up in his turn and started
for the door, she said humbly: 'I did try to read
the papers, and I was going to get Juffrouw de
Waal to help me, but Peta was there—and your
parents were away from home. There is no one else
I can ask about last night, so please will you...?
I'm sorry about last night.'

He came back at once and sat down opposite her. 'One is apt to forget that your Dutch is fragmental,' he observed in a faintly amused voice. 'There was a multiple crash—a tanker jack-knifed and caught a car as it was passing on the fast lane. The cars behind couldn't stop in time—there were thirty or so cars damaged, I believe.'

She asked impatiently: 'But you? What about you?'

He gave her a quick, hooded glance. 'There was a fair amount of first aid to be done,' he observed mildly.

'Couldn't you have telephoned?'

He smiled faintly at some private joke. 'No. There was a great deal to do.' And before she could speak again, he was on his way to the door again. 'And now I really must get those notes written up.'

Lavinia dressed defiantly and rather grandly for dinner that evening. Mijnheer de Wit and his wife were coming, and another surgeon whom she had met briefly at their wedding, and she had taken the precaution of inviting Sibby's student friend as well as a young cousin of Radmer's, still in his first year at Leiden medical school.

She was downstairs long before anyone else, wandering restlessly from room to room in her pink-patterned organza dress, the pearls clasped round her throat, her hair carefully coiled. She was giving the dining table a quite unnecessary inspection when Radmer looked in.

'Very nice,' he commented, and she wondered if he was referring to the table, the beautiful room, or her own person. She played safe. 'White linen always looks perfect,' she assured him earnestly, 'and I thought the pink roses would be just right with the silver and glass.'

He left the door and strolled across the room to where she was standing. He was in a dinner jacket and looked somehow taller and broader than ever. A few inches from her he stopped, half smiling. 'I must admit,' he said suavely, 'that considering your low——your very low opinion of me as a husband, you have excelled yourself in the management of our home, and since I am now quite beyond the pale, I might, if I may mix my metaphors, as well be hanged for a sheep as a lamb.'

She felt herself held fast and pulled close by one great arm, while his other hand lifted her chin. He kissed her fiercely, and when she opened her mouth to speak, he kissed her again, but this time gently, still holding her tightly.

'You know,' he told her, 'I've been wanting to do that, and now that I have I feel much better.'

'Oh,' said Lavinia in a very small voice. 'Why?'

His smile mocked her. 'For all the wrong reasons, my dear.'

She hadn't known what he was going to say, but she had hoped for something else without realizing it, so that sudden tears pricked her eyelids and filled her throat. His arms had slackened a little. She tore herself away from him and rushed to the door, to collide with Peta and Sibby, on the point of coming in. Lavinia caught a glimpse of their surprised faces as she ran up the staircase.

She mustn't cry, she told herself in her bedroom. She dabbed her eyes, powdered her nose and drank some water, and then, with her chin well up, went downstairs again, where she joined the others in the sitting-room, making light conversation as though her life depended upon it, and not once looking at Radmer, or for that matter, speaking to him.

The evening should have been a failure, she had felt convinced that it would be, but it was nothing of the sort; dinner was superb, the talk lighthearted and never flagging, and the party, adjourning to the drawing-room afterwards, broke up only after its members had expressed themselves enchanted with their evening. Lavinia, standing on the top step outside the front door, waving good-byes, felt no enchantment, however. The evening for her had been endless; all she had wanted to do was to have gone somewhere quiet and had a good cry.

The girls went to bed almost at once, and pausing only to make sure that the dining-room had been set to rights, and plump up a few cushions in the drawing-room, Lavinia made haste to follow them, bidding Radmer a subdued good night as she went, not waiting to see if he had anything else to say to her but his own quiet good night.

She managed to avoid Radmer during the next few days, coming down to breakfast a little earlier than anyone else, so that she excused herself almost as soon as he got to the table, on the plea of having to see Mevrouw Pette about something or other, and if he came home for tea, there were the girls to act as an unconscious barrier between them, and as for the evenings, if he didn't go to his study, she engrossed herself in letter writing or grocery lists so that she wasn't called upon to take more than a desultory part in the conversation around her. She felt rather pleased with herself on the whole; she had remained pleasant and friendly, she considered, just as she always had been. Certainly there had been one or two small lapses; she preferred not to remember them. But she didn't know how pale she had become, causing her to look positively plain as well as sad, nor did she

know how false her gaiety was and how stiff she
was with Radmer.

It was a week after the dinner party when she
came home from her Dutch lesson at lunch time to
find a worried Mevrouw Pette, and because there
was no one there to help them understand each
other, it took her a few minutes to get the gist of
what the housekeeper was saying.

'The girls,' said Mevrouw Pette, anxiously.
'They came home not half an hour ago, *mevrouw*,
and they went to Sibendina's room and talked, and
then they asked me for coffee, and when I asked
if they couldn't wait until you came home at lunch
time they said no, they had to go out. I gave them
their coffee, *mevrouw*—I hope I did right?—and a
little later, I came into the hall to fetch the tray and
they were going out of the house, and they each
had a case with them. They didn't see me, but I
heard Sibendina talking about the train and the
Zuidplein and the metro.' She broke off and cast
a worried look at Lavinia. 'There is a shopping
centre at the Zuidplein, *mevrouw*, but that is in
Rotterdam—there is also a metro there.'

Lavinia had gone rather white. She hadn't followed Mevrouw Pette's speech easily and for the
moment she was totally bewildered. 'Are you
sure?' she asked. 'I mean, there are masses of
shops in Amsterdam, why should they go there?

I'll look in their rooms, perhaps they've left a note—they must have left something. Will you look downstairs?'

There were no notes, but some clothes had gone; night clothes, toilet things, undies. Lavinia raced downstairs again and telephoned the school. It had been one of the mornings when Peta went with Sibby to join her class. Neither of them would normally come home until lunch time. While she waited to be connected she remembered unhappily that Peta had asked her only the previous evening if she were happy, and when she had assured her that she was, her sister had said forcefully: 'Well, Sibby and I don't think you are—and Radmer isn't either.' She had run away to her room then, and Lavinia had thought it wiser to say nothing more about it. Now she wished that she had.

The authoritative voice which answered her query about the girls assured her that there had been no reason why they had left school early— indeed, no one, it seemed, had been aware of their absence. The voice, speaking very concise English, wanted to know if they were ill.

'No,' said Lavinia. 'I'll telephone you later, if I may.'

She went to her room then, found her handbag, stuffed some money into it, and without bothering to see if she were tidy enough to go out, went to find Mevrouw Pette. 'I'll go after them,' she explained to that good lady. 'I'll go to Rotterdam just in case they went there. Will you get a taxi for me? Perhaps they haven't gone there…'

'I heard them,' said Mevrouw Pette. 'Shall I tell the Professor?'

Lavinia shook her head. 'I'm not quite sure where he is, and he's got that very important postmortem today. Besides, the girls may be back long before he comes home. If they are, don't let them go out again, Mevrouw Pette, and if I don't find them, I'll telephone you later.' She added hopefully: 'It's just a joke, I expect—how did they look? Did you see them laughing?'

Mevrouw Pette shook her head. 'They were very earnest.' She frowned. 'And you, *mevrouw*, you have had no lunch—I will fetch you some coffee.'

But Lavinia shook her head; she had wasted quite enough time already and she had no idea how frequently the trains ran to Rotterdam or how long they took over the forty-five-mile journey, and even when she got there, she still had to find Zuidplein.

She sat in the taxi, fretting, and when she reached the Central Station wasted a few precious minutes finding the ticket office and the right platform. She arrived on it to see the tail end of a Rotterdam-bound train disappearing from sight.

The trains ran frequently, though; she watched the outskirts of Amsterdam slide away and reviewed the situation, but somehow, because she was tired and frightened about the girls, her brain refused to function. She stared out of the window, seeing nothing of the view from it, her head quite empty.

At Rotterdam station she wandered around for a short time, trying out her Dutch without much success, until a kindly ticket collector pointed out the way to the metro and told her to get on it and stay there until it stopped at the end of its run—that would be Zuidplein, he explained carefully.

It was easy after that. She left the metro thankfully, but dismayed that it was more than two hours since she had left home, and for all she knew, she reminded herself, she had come on a wild goose chase.

She followed everyone else hurrying off the platform and disappearing through various exits, and after several false starts, went down a flight of stairs and pushed open the heavy doors at the bottom, to find herself in a vast hall, brightly lighted and noisy with the hum of a great many people all talking at once. It was lined with shops of every sort and size, and Lavinia started to walk towards the centre, appalled at the prospect of trying to find anyone in such a crowded place.

She turned her back on the big stores of Vroom and Dreesman, which took up the whole of one end of the enormous place, and began to revolve slowly, getting her bearings. She was two thirds of the way round when she saw Radmer standing a little way off, watching her.

She didn't know how her joy at seeing him there showed on her worried face. She ran towards him without a moment's hesitation, bumping into the shoppers milling around her as she went, and when she reached him, she clutched at his jacket rather in the manner of someone half drowned hanging on to a providential tree trunk.

'Radmer!' she babbled. 'How did you know? How did you get here so quickly? They're here somewhere; Mevrouw Pette heard them talking—I don't know why they had to come so far...I got on the first train I could—they couldn't have got here much before I did...well,' she paused and added worriedly: 'It must be hours by now. Radmer...' She stopped to gulp back all the terrifying thoughts she longed to voice.

He had her hands in his, nice and firm and secure, and although he looked grave, he smiled a little at her. 'How fortunate that I should have gone home early—I wanted to talk to you. Mevrouw Pette told me what had happened and I drove down; I had just got there when I saw you. And don't worry, Lavinia, it shouldn't be too difficult to find them if they're here.' His voice was comfortably matter-of-fact as he tucked an arm in hers and went on calmly: 'I think our best plan will be to walk right round this place, not too fast, just in the hope of meeting them. If we have no luck, we'll think of what is to be done.'

It took them almost an hour, for there were lanes of shops leading from the centre hall, and these led in turn to other lanes. There was even a market, packed with shoppers, and any number of snack bars and cafés. At any other time, with nothing on her mind, Lavinia would have found it all rather fun and enjoyed exploring the shops; now, looking in all directions at once, she hardly saw them.

Back where they had started from, Radmer said easily: 'Now, supposing we go round once more, but this time we'll look in every shop.' He smiled down at her. 'We can ask in all the most likely ones if anyone has seen them—you must tell me what they were wearing. Are you tired, Lavinia?'

She was, but she shook her head. She had hardly spoken as they had walked round, but now she said in a polite little voice: 'No, not in the least, thank you. Where shall we start?'

He took her arm again. 'What about Hema?' he asked. 'Isn't that the sort of shop they would enjoy looking round?' He started across the shopping centre, skirting the small, circular boutiques, chic confectioners and knick-knack shops which occupied its hub. They were almost across it when she felt his fingers tighten on her arm. 'There they are!' his voice was quiet, but she could hear the relief in it. 'Over there, in that teashop.'

It was another circular structure, glass and wood, with a tiny terrace built around it, its interior brilliantly lighted. Lavinia could see Sibby and Peta, their two heads close together over a table in the window, deep in conversation. Even at that distance she saw that although they were in earnest conversation, they didn't look dejected.

Radmer was walking her briskly towards the teashop. At its door he said calmly: 'Go and join them, my dear, I'll bring you a cup of tea.' His eyes met hers briefly and he smiled as she made her way through the crowded little place and sat down opposite Sibby. She was quite unprepared for her: 'Oh, good—we've been praying ever so hard that you'd come,' and Peta chimed in with: 'Did Radmer come after you, Lavinia?'

She nodded, not daring to speak, for if she had done so, she would have burst into tears and spoilt her image of stepmother and elder sister for ever. Fortunately Radmer joined them then, sitting down beside Sibby and facing her.

'I'm glad we found you,' he observed in a cheerful voice, and Sibendina said at once: 'So are we, Papa. We were just wondering what we should do next—we counted on you coming after us; at least, we guessed Lavinia would, and if you came after her…it was a gamble.'

'Why did you run away, my dears?' His voice was placid with no hint of anger.

Peta answered him. 'It seemed a good idea. We didn't do it on the spur of the moment, you know; we talked about it for days. We had a reason, didn't we, Sibby?' She paused, but he made no effort to prompt her, instead he put milk and sugar in Lavinia's cup and put it into her hands.

'Drink up, dear girl,' he urged her, and she drank obediently, swallowing her tears with the tea, still not daring to trust her voice.

'It isn't our business,' began Peta awkwardly, and looked at Radmer to see if he was going to agree with her, but all he did was to smile faintly, so that she felt encouraged to go on. 'Sibby and I—we thought that if we did something really drastic, like almost drowning, or being knocked down by a car or running away, you would both have to help each other and it would make you fond of each other, because you love Sibby and Lavinia loves me, and that would make you understand each other and share the same feelings…' She looked at him anxiously. 'Perhaps that's not very clear?'

'On the contrary, I get your point very clearly.' He had stretched out a hand and taken Lavinia's small clenched fist in his, but he hadn't looked at her.

'We decided we'd run away,' said Sibby, taking up the tale, 'because we both swim too well to drown easily, and to walk in front of a car—just like that—' she waved an expressive hand, 'we found that we were unable to do that—besides, we might have been killed instead of just a little wounded and then our idea would have been wasted. So we ran away, and if you had not come after us we would have known that you did not love each other.' She beamed at them both. 'I explain badly, but you must agree that it was a good idea.'

Lavinia found her voice then, a little gruff but quite steady. 'But, my dears, supposing we hadn't found you in this crowd of people? Whatever would I do without you both?'

Sibby said softly: 'It would have been OK. You have Papa, you belong...'

Lavinia clenched her hands tightly so that the knuckles showed white. For a few moments she forgot where she was, she forgot, too, her well-ordered upbringing which had taught her so painstakingly never to display her feelings in public and always to speak in a well-modulated voice. She said loudly and rather fast: 'You're wrong, I don't belong. It's your papa who belongs—to his work and your mother—or her memory. He—he...' She stopped, appalled at her words, to look at their faces, Sibby and Peta expectant and inquiring, Radmer, daring to lounge in his chair like that and actually smiling... She glared at him, muttering, snatched up her handbag, pushed her stool violently away and made for the kiosk's second door. She had no idea where she was going and she really didn't care. She hurried blindly ahead, quite unaware that Radmer was right behind her.

The two girls watched their progress with interest until Sibby said: 'It has worked, Peta, I do believe it has! In a few minutes they will have what you call a showdown, although I cannot think that this is a very good place.' She looked around her. 'There is no romance here.' She shrugged her shoulders and grinned at Peta. 'They will be back, but not yet—we have time for one of those delicious ices—the one with the nuts and chocolate.'

They went arm-in-arm to the counter to give their order.

Lavinia walked very fast through the throng of shoppers, colliding with one or other of them continuously and apologizing carefully in English each time she did it. She wanted to lose herself as quickly as possible, although common sense was already asking the nagging question where she should go and what would she do when she got there. And what would happen to the girls? Of Radmer she refused to think. She shut her eyes for an instant on the memory of his smile and bumped into a stout matron with a shopping basket. She was close to Vroom and Dreesman now, so she plunged into the mass of people thronging its open shop front, and allowed herself to be pushed and shoved from one counter to the other, getting lightning glimpses of watches, gloves, tights and costume jewellery. She managed to stop here, and stood staring at the bead necklaces and bangles and diamanté brooches until the salesgirl looked at her inquiringly, so that she felt she should walk on, into a corner this time where there was a circular stand with a display of scarves on it. For the moment there was no one there, so she stood forlornly, staring at the bright silky things, her mind quite empty.

'Darling,' said the professor very quietly in her ear, and clamped a hand on to her shoulder. Lavinia cried 'Oh!' so loudly that a smartly dressed woman who had paused to finger the scarves gave her a sharp look and moved away.

'I don't think that this is the ideal spot for a man to tell his wife that he loves her...'

She choked on a sob and then said woodenly, addressing the merchandise before her: 'But you don't...'

She was swivelled round in gentle hands and held fast, so that all she could see was a portion of waistcoat and the glimpse of a white silk shirt. She muttered into it: 'You told me, you know you told me—that I could never come between you and Helga.'

A finger tilted her chin so that she was forced to look into his face, and the expression on it made her catch her breath. 'Oh, yes, I said that, and it was true, you know—for how could you come between me and someone who is no longer there—has not been there for very many years? Helga means nothing to me, my darling—nor did she for the greater part of our life together. One day I'll tell you about that, but not now. We have other, more important things to talk of.'

She stared up into his calm, assured face. 'But when we married—no, before that, when you asked me to marry you—you told me that you didn't love me. You said you wanted a friendly relationship, you said...'

He kissed her to a halt. 'Quite right. What a fool a man can be, for even then the idea of not marrying you was quite insupportable, even though I pretended to myself that I was going to marry you for a number of very sensible reasons. And my darling, you were so very careful to let me know as often as possible that you wanted it that way, too. But that night at the farm, when I saw you standing at the bottom of the stairs, waiting for me in the smoke, I had to admit to myself that I loved you too much to go on as we had intended—either I would have to tell you that or keep out of your way.'

'You made me drive the Bentley,' she reminded him, following her own train of thought, 'and I was terrified, and when you came to that house you were quite beastly.'

He pulled her closer so that a young woman with a pushchair could pass them. 'My darling, I wanted to wring your neck and take you in my arms and tell you how wonderful you were and how you were driving me slowly mad,'

She said idiotically: 'I bought those dresses and had my hair done...'

'And I wanted to tell you that you were the most beautiful girl in the world, but I was afraid to in case I frightened you away.' He bent to kiss her. 'I never thought to love like this,' he told her. 'Nothing means anything any more if you aren't with me.' He paused and smiled at a massive woman in Zeeuwse costume who was edging past them. 'The other night, when I came home late and I knew that you loved me...'

'I never said a word!'

'You said a great many words. You were very cross, my darling.'

'I was angry because I was frightened.'

'I know.' He kissed her again, not minding in the least that a small boy and two girls had stopped to watch them.

Lavinia caught their fascinated eyes and went pink. 'Don't think I don't like being kissed, Radmer darling, but isn't it rather public?'

He looked around him. 'You are probably right, my love. Let us go back to Sibby and Peta, who are probably congratulating each other and making themselves sick on ice-cream.'

'Well, they did what they set out to do; I mean, running away like that, it did make us come together.'

They began to walk, not hurrying in the least, back to the teashop.

'Why do you suppose I came home early?' asked Radmer.

'I don't know—tell me,'

'Because I couldn't go on any longer as we were. I was going to ask you if you could forgive me for being so blind, and start all over again.'

She stopped to smile at him. 'Oh, yes, please, Radmer,' and she looked away quickly from his eyes. 'Oh, look, there are the girls, watching.'

They both waved, and Radmer said: 'I once said that you were a girl who would never reach for the moon, dearest Lavinia, but you will have no need to do that, for I intend to give it to you—I'll throw in the sun and the stars for good measure.'

'How nice,' said Lavinia, 'but I'd just as soon have you, my darling.'

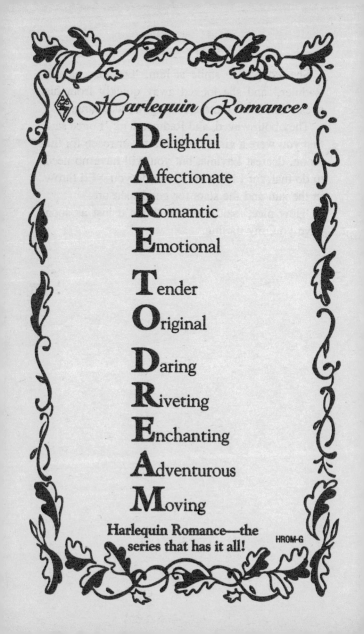

Harlequin Romance®

Delightful

Affectionate

Romantic

Emotional

Tender

Original

Daring

Riveting

Enchanting

Adventurous

Moving

Harlequin Romance—the
series that has it all!

HROM-G